Westward Wanderers

-BOOK THREE-

SEASON

OF

FLIGHT

Angela Castillo (signature)

D1739132

Angela Castillo

To Rosie and Cherie.
My sisters, my dear friends.

Books by Angela Castillo

Texas Women of Spirit Series:
The River Girl's Song
The Comanche Girl's Prayer
The Saloon Girl's Journey
The River Girl's Christmas

The Miss Main Series:
Secondhand Secrets
Blessed Arrangements
Inn Dependence

The Westward Wanderers Series:
Where He Leads
The Dawn Wakers
Season of Flight

I

Sunset Branches

Branches swayed as though a sudden storm swept through them. A shower of petals, soft and white as cream floating in a milk barrel, settled on Fern's hair and shoulders. Her glance shifted to the limb above, where one slender bare foot landed, followed by a second. Her sister sank into a fork in the limbs, her skirts settling around her.

"Want to climb higher?" Iris asked, her cheeks bright. "The leaves are too thick for much of a view now, but the blossoms are glorious."

"I believe I'll stay where I am." Fern gripped sturdy limbs on either side of her perch, repressing a gasp when her sister's movements shook the tree harder. She and Iris had climbed this apple tree every year on the anniversary of the day their family had arrived, worn to rags, from the Oregon trail. Farm work kept Fern limber and strong, but each year she was a bit less daring.

Iris, bravest of the four sisters in every way, always climbed the highest, until the branches became too spindly to hold even her slight figure.

The ladies in the town of Cottage Grove would have been scandalized to vapors to see Fern and Iris behaving in such a fashion. After all, two grown women of twenty-one and twenty-three did not belong in a tree.

Founder girls never worried about the opinions of others. As Mrs. Founder always said, "God watches our every act, and that's a heap of watching. We don't need to worry about any other set of eyes, even if they happen to be in the same head as a spiteful tongue."

Iris dangled her legs over the side, kicking leaves with her bare toes. "Oh, it's lovely to be free of flannel petticoats for the summer."

"They're awfully cumbersome." Fern wiggled her toes. "Peony said we ought to find an Indian to sell us deerskin leggings."

Iris laughed. "Silly Peony. She'd have a fit if I paraded around the house in such outlandish clothes, even if it was her suggestion. Still, they'd be heaven for horseback riding. Maybe I will buy some. If I ever meet up with an Indian."

"Leggings would be handy for working the fields during early plowing," Fern said. "They'd protect us from thorns and snakes much better than our flimsy cotton underthings. We could wear them under our skirts. No one would even know."

"There's a thought." Iris scooted down from her branch to alight beside Fern. She threw her head back, her loose, dark hair streaming behind her. Closing her eyes, she inhaled deeply. "Isn't spring wonderful?"

Fern gazed at the snowy blooms surrounding them. The scent, with faint promises of the fruit to come, filled the air. Tiny blossoms rested in her sister's hair, making her resemble a member of the Fair Folk even more than usual.

"I always embrace it, even though it's our busiest time." Fern plucked a blossom from its twig and twisted it between her thumb and forefinger so it spun like a dancing lady's skirt. "It's really like magic, how everything knows what time is safe to open and grow. The sun coaxes the baby animals from their mother's wombs, out to play."

"Spring is when I feel the closest to God," Iris murmured. "The season serves to remind me; He makes all things new, after the cold and darkness of winter."

Fern smiled. Iris always brought things back to God. Though Granny, her mother, and the four sisters all held a steadfast faith, Iris's relationship was of a different nature entirely. She heard God speak to her directly, and she knew things about people, secrets impossible to divine on her own. She'd had to be careful who she told about this ability. Many people, even members of their church, believed such powers were from the Devil, though the words Iris heard brought life and goodness. Iris learned from an early age to hold most of these thoughts inside, only speaking of them with her family, or writing in journals, which she kept stacked in the loft the four sisters shared.

Fern believed her sister's divine gifting, not only because the discernments she uttered were found to be true, but because Fern had also heard the voice of God in her own heart at times. But not as often as Iris.

"Miss Fern! Miss Iris!" A boy's voice floated up through the boughs.

"That'll be Robbie." Iris sat up straight. "His father took him to town today, and he promised to check for mail."

"You'd better get after the bees anyway," said Fern. She inched towards the trunk, freeing her dress when the cloth snagged on the bark.

"You don't have to keep climbing this tree with me anymore if you don't want to," Iris said. "Peony and Myrtle haven't come for ages."

Fern's hand slipped, and a sharp twig tore a thin crimson line through her skin. "I wouldn't miss it for the world," she said through gritted teeth.

Iris raised an eyebrow.

Fern stared through the leafy bower.

Robbie, the fifteen-year-old neighbor boy, grinned up at her. "I knew you and your sisters were unusual," he said, "but I never expected to see you up a tree."

"And why ever not?" she teased. "Now close your eyes and turn around. Ascending from trees is not always a decent business."

Robbie did as he was told.

The ground wasn't far, but Fern slipped and crashed on her knees, landing in a heap of skirts. As she rose and dusted herself off, Iris lighted beside her, as graceful as a dandelion seed floating on the wind.

"I'm off to the bees." Iris darted away through the orchard. She was never one for company, though Robbie was almost like kin to the Founder family.

Robbie held out his hand to Fern. "Did you hurt yourself?"

Fern grabbed his wrist and hauled herself up. "I don't think so." She brushed off the twigs and leaves clinging to her skirt. "Though I probably look a sight. Since Iris is checking the bees, I'd better go see if Mother needs help with supper."

"Mrs. Founder is the one who sent me to fetch you," said Robbie.

They strolled through rows of blossoming trees. Evening birds swooped after insect suppers, and chipmunks scurried on last minute evening errands.

"I brought a letter from town." Robbie shoved his hands in his pockets and kicked a little rock, which bounded through last fall's leaves. "After your mother read it, she told me to come out here and fetch you."

"Who was it from?" Fern's heart beat a little faster. She'd never outgrown the girlish excitement any news brought, especially here at the farm, where deviations to routine were rare.

"Dunno." He shrugged. "She didn't seem sad or anything."

"Well, that's good, I suppose."

They reached the squat, simple farmhouse the Founder women had built mostly with their own hands.

"Stay for supper?" Fern asked Robbie.

His eyes lit up, but he looked away. "I'd better get home to Ma. Still have chores to do."

"Have you heard from your sister?" Fern hadn't seen her dear friend, Ellie, since her wedding in the Founder's house at Christmas.

Robbie smiled. "Oh yes. She and Thaddeus are doing well. They plan to visit sometime in early May."

"That will be nice for your mother. And all of you."

He paused and brushed a hand over his face, giving that quick, shifty look a boy made when trying to hide emotion. "Yes, we miss her. But she's happy. Mother keeps hoping for a baby."

"How is the church going?"

"We visited a month back." He grimaced. "My shoes were tight. But Thaddeus's sermons don't stretch on for ages like the pastor in Cottage Grove. When he talks, I feel like God is right there in the room."

Fern giggled. "That's how you should feel, silly."

Robbie stared at the path before them. "No. I mean . . . the pastor in town talks like God is a big scary giant, waiting to stomp me into the ground the moment I do something wrong. When Thaddeus preaches, I think of God as a father who cares about me."

"Thaddeus is right," Fern murmured. "God would leave ninety-nine sheep just to find one that's lost. Does that sound like someone who would stomp you into the ground, Robbie?"

"No." Robbie's chipped front tooth glinted in the sunlight. He tipped his Stetson, so battered and misshapen it could scarcely be called a hat. "I'd better get home to supper, Miss Fern."

"Goodnight, Robbie."

As usual, Granny rocked on the front porch with the ancient gray cat, Bartholomew, curled up in her lap. She appeared to be napping, but when Fern walked by, her eyes, bright as raindrops, snapped open. "Hey there, Fernie. Did that boy bring us new 'lasses?"

"We have plenty in the house. I'm sure you can have molasses on your biscuits tonight, Granny," said Fern.

"How can I have 'mo lasses when I haven't had any in the first place?" Though it was a tired old joke Granny had repeated many times, this one came as a grumble.

"I'll hurry right in and see if Peoney has set the table," Fern said.

"See that you do." Granny swept the cat from her lap and rose from her seat, the rockers slapping against the porch.

Fern stepped into the house. Splashes of dusky sunlight

greeted her from the windows, and fresh breezes floated in from open windows, tugging on the quilts and crocheted doilies that covered tables and furniture in the front room. *Peony and Myrtle must've aired out the house today.* Fern loved the first airing of the house. It seemed to chase the dark and gloom of winter away, announcing once and for all spring was here, and nothing could stop its breezy advance.

Past the large open front room was the door to the dining area, with the cozy kitchen beside that. Peony, the second oldest sister after Myrtle, was placing folded napkins by each earthenware plate.

"You're in late," she scolded playfully. "Mother's taking johnnycakes from the oven and the ham's glazed. Got a nice pot of beans on to simmer as well."

"Sounds lovely." Fern went to the side door that led to the yard to wash up at the little outdoor pump.

Peony and Myrtle preferred to stay inside and handle the housekeeping, while Mother, Iris and Fern took care of the bees and livestock. Everyone pitched in for planting and harvests, and several hired men cared for the massive fields, and the orchards of fruit and nut trees that stretched far as the eye could see. Altogether fifty acres made up the Founder's farm, more than half tilled and cleared by the women, a patch at a time. Fern had vague memories of following behind Mother's bustling skirts when she was only five, gathering rocks in her little bucket to dump in handy ditches.

Myrtle burst through the door, a flurry of energy as usual. Her cheeks were round and rosy, and her hair bobbed about her shoulders in natural, springy curls. Like the other Founder women, she rarely bothered to pin her hair up formally unless heading to town or hosting company, though she was the oldest daughter at thirty.

The sisters were far from uncivilized, with all their wild appearances. Mother had taken great pains to teach them the social graces, and they could all pour tea and walk with the mincing steps required to balance books on their heads if they felt like it. But when alone they put these formalities to the side.

None were married, though eager prospects for all four sisters could form a line to the next county.

"Men hankerin' after your beauty and the goodliness of our farm," Mother often sniffed, though she'd broken her own share of middle-aged bachelor's hearts.

Peony brought in Grandma, who shuffled across the wooden floorboards like an aged tortoise, casting appraising glances from side to side.

"Sideboards need dusting," she muttered as Peony helped her to her accustomed chair.

"Dusted them yesterday, Granny," said Peony, giving Fern an amused glance.

"They're dusty, and that's all there is to it," Granny snapped back.

Peony ignored the old woman and went to stand behind her

own chair.

Myrtle glanced out the window. "Waiting on Iris," she said, twisting a silver ring around her finger.

Myrtle was the only one who'd been engaged. Charles had died in a distant battlefield in a place called Gettysburg two years ago. She'd recovered, if anyone could recover from such a thing. But her smile never flashed as quickly as it had before.

Mother caried in a platter of steaming ham. She glanced around the table at her daughters. "Iris coming?"

"With the bees," Fern replied.

"Very well. She can say her own grace," said Mother. They'd learned long ago that a dinner waiting for Iris would usually be served cold. No one minded. She went by her own path and her own timing. It was the way she'd been since a child.

Mother never scolded her. She always said, "The more space you give a child to grow, the more unique a vessel you will end up with."

And Iris was unique. With her grey eyes and cloud of dark hair, she'd broken more hearts than the other Founder women combined. But she was a wild, wandering soul, and though distantly polite, lovesick suiters rarely received her attention.

Fern had her share of admirers, but she'd never been able to turn them away with the finesse of her sister. At first she'd guilted herself with notions of the sorrows they must take with them, and the possible damage to their manly egos. After a while she'd learned not to take these to heart. "Don't bother," her mother would say, "plenty of silly simpering girls exist to snatch them up in a hummingbird's wink."

Mother gave a short grace, and then the family began to eat.

Fern slathered butter on a thick slice of bread, contemplating the gleaming yellow swirls. "Mother, Robbie said you wanted to tell me about a letter he brought. Somehow, I completely forgot on the way from the giant apple tree to the house."

Everyone at the table chuckled. Fern always forgot things.

"Yes." Mother passed a bowl of peas to Granny, who made a face and shoved the bowl towards Myrtle. "A rancher in Emerald City heard about our bees. He'd like one of our farmhands to bring down a few hives and show him how to tend them. He's offering twenty-five dollars."

"Twenty-five dollars?" Peony's deep blue eyes widened. "We could use that for a good heifer with money to spare. These spring calves are probably the last these old ladies will give."

"That's what I was thinking." Mother's forehead furrowed. "Of course, we'll send Carl to deliver them."

"Carl doesn't know the first thing about bees," Iris said as she came through the door, drying her hands on her apron.

Fern poked at her peas. Carl was the Founder farm's oldest hand. He'd been with them for fourteen years, had built a small cabin on the property, and was pretty much an adopted uncle. The Founders trusted him like family, but Iris was right, he didn't know much about bees.

"We have those small hives we've been cultivating," said Iris.

"Would there be enough?"

Fern counted on her fingers. "There's seven left over from the ones we sold to the Callahan farm. Five would do well, don't you agree, Mother?"

Mother exhaled, blowing the ribbons of her dinner cap into whirling dervishes. "Yes, five should do well, and the heat hasn't landed. The bees can keep the honey cool on the journey. I'd say the trip to Emerald City won't take longer than two days."

"Emerald City," Myrtle said. "Isn't that by the coast?"

Mother gave a tiny smile. "I believe so."

Fern's heart fluttered, and she dropped her fork. "Oh, Mother, you want me to go, don't you? I've always wanted to see the ocean! Carl can look after me. I know bees better than cows and cats. I'll make sure they reach their new home safely." She rushed up from her seat, nearly overturning her teacup, and hugged her mother. "You are so good to me!"

"Yes, yes, I want you to go with Carl." Mother laughed and returned the hug. "It's time you see more of the world you dream about so much. I'd send Iris, but I think she'd run off and become a pirate."

Iris made a face. "I have no desire to teach some strange man about bees. Doubt he'll listen to a woman anyway." She glanced at Fern. "Sorry, Fern. Maybe he will."

"It doesn't matter." Fern twirled, her skirts fluffing out like ruffled chicken feathers. "I'm going to see the ocean!"

2
Rocky Arrival

Carl's voice, sweet and sure, though cracked a bit by age, carried out over the road.

"The golden hours, on angel wings,

Flew o'er me and my dearie;

For dear to me, as light and life,

Was my sweet Highland Mary!"

Fern blinked and stirred, then sat up in the wagon bed. Her hair fell in untidy strands over her forehead, and she tucked them behind her ears.

They'd traveled for two days and were on the third morning now. Her body was numb all over from never-ending jolts and bumps.

For the first hours of that morning, she'd ridden in the front with Carl, but after a while she'd decided to take a nap. Old quilts piled in the wagon bed had made a perfect nest; shielding her from the worst of the lurches.

The bees, contained in five wooden crates behind her, buzzed in an urgent plea for freedom.

"Don't worry," she whispered. "We'll be at your new home before you know it. I hope Iris is wrong and they'll listen to instructions and take care of you. They're paying an awful lot of money." She patted a box. "Of course, you ladies can take care of yourselves. I'm sure you'll fly away and find a nice hollow tree in the forest if your caretakers don't suit you."

The wagon came to a halt, as did the lilting Scottish ballad.

Is it lunchtime already? I must have slept the morning away. Fern stretched and rose until her back brushed the wagon cover. She crept to the end of the bed, taking care to avoid the crates of bees, as a sudden kick would make them fractious. After grabbing the lunch pail, packed that morning by the kindly woman from the boardinghouse, she went to the front of the wagon.

Carl was running his hands over the fetlock of Tom, one of the dappled old cart horses. Carl looked up, his eyes crinkling at the corners. "Hey, there, Lassie. Did you get a good sleep?"

Fern smiled at the term Carl used for her and her sisters. Even though Carl's parents had come over from the "old country" as he called Scotland, years before he was born, he still talked with a bit of a brogue. His bright red beard was streaked with white. The rare times he'd removed his floppy old hat revealed a shining bald scalp and large ears that stuck out like the gnomes in the fairy books Mother read aloud to the family on chilly evenings. He always had a kind word and a merry attitude, and Fern loved him almost as much as her sisters.

"I had a lovely nap." She held up the pail. "Are you ready for lunch?

"This spring air makes me frightfully hungry." He gave the container in her hand an appraising glance.

"Me too." Fern pulled off the lid. "Let's see. Apples. Cheese sandwiches. Boiled eggs. And a jar of milk."

He smacked his lips. "And God's glorious earth to admire while we eat."

They spread a quilt over a grassy patch on the roadside. The blades were lush and thick as the carpet of royalty. Fields spread out on both sides, not a house or tree in sight, only acres and acres of spring flowers in golds, blues, and purples. Their intoxicating perfume filled the air.

Carl nodded towards the wagon. "I bet your bees are getting anxious with all these flowers waitin' to be visited."

"I'm sure." Fern rapped her egg against the pail's rim and peeled off the shell in satisfying strips. "They don't have to wait much longer now. I hope they take well to their new home."

"Aw, they'll do fine," said Carl. "Especially with your instruction and care."

"No telling," Fern replied. "One can never know with bees,

but that's what makes them exciting."

Carl settled back on the quilt. "Whoo whee, what a day! Makes you glad to be alive, does it not?"

Fern wriggled her toes, bare and free of pinching leather and itchy stockings. "I'm always glad to be alive."

Carl patted her hand. "So young. Haven't seen too much heartache yet. But that's fine, my dear. Hope you always feel that way."

"I'm blessed beyond measure, Carl, to have a family who loves me and God's grace in my life," said Fern. "But I wasn't trying to downplay the hardship of others."

"'Tis a marvelous attitude," said Carl. "Meself, I have few complaints to mention, especially since I came to live on the Founder farm."

After they'd finished lunch and packed up the supplies, Fern reluctantly put on her shoes. She walked beside the buckboard for a spell, allowing the spring breeze to waft through her waist-length hair. The sun climbed through the sky in a fiery blaze, burning off clouds in its wake.

Carl halted the wagon "See that smoke?" He pointed to a thin gray wisp rising lazily in the distance. "We should reach Emerald City in the next hour, I think."

Fern climbed aboard. "I suppose I should try to arrange my hair a bit more respectably."

"Aye." Carl gave her a slanted glance. "You don't want these folks thinkin' you're a lass of twelve."

"Is that how I look, Carl?"

Carl didn't answer, but the corner of his mouth twitched. Sometimes it was hard to tell when he was teasing.

Rocks dotted the clay road, and the buckboard pitched up and down. Carl leaned over the edge. "Have to watch for these larger rocks on the road here. You'd think someone would bring a team of oxen out here to haul some of these off, considerin' this is one of the oldest towns in Oregon."

"You'd think," Fern yelled as a wheel bumped over a particularly big stone. "Maybe they only care about boats."

Tom snorted and reared up suddenly, loose leather straps sliding down his back. The other horse, Sue, whinnied, loud and long.

"What's happening?" Fern cried as both horses plunged and bucked.

"Gotta be a snake," Carl yelled, twisting the reins around his work-gnarled hands.

The wagon shuddered and rumbled down the hill, faster and faster.

Fern's teeth rattled and trees on the roadside became green blurs. The creaks and clatters hurt her ears.

"Woah there, Tom, the snake's far gone now!" Carl yelled. "Woah, there, Sue!"

"I don't think they can stop!" he shouted to Fern. He bounced high in his seat, once, twice. A third pitch sent him over the side. His head bobbed from the edge, round face contorted and red. "Fern! My–hands! Can't get–free!"

Bile rose in Fern's throat, and she gasped for breath. She threw herself to Carl's side of the wagon and drew out the long-bladed knife she always kept in a sheath at her waist.

Carl's yells were drowned out by the screams of the horses, who ran as though the wagon was a monster set to devour them.

Fern tried to grab for the reins, but the thick leather was tight and heavy, and the rough sides stung her hands. *If I cut them, I'll never get control of the horses. If I don't, Carl will die.*

She sawed through the reins.

Carl's head disappeared as he fell away from the wagon. His shouts weakened behind her.

Relieved of his weight, the horses caught a fresh wind. The ground evened out, and they continued to run, foam dripping from their sides.

Sue took a sharp turn, as if to chide Tom for his decision to bolt. Fern dropped the knife and clutched for the rough wooden boards, but only grasped emptiness. The ground rushed up to meet her like a rolling brown wave and her head met something hard with a sickening crunch.

###

"Ma'am. Ma'am."

The voice pressed through her dreams, like an incessant cow lowing for its dinner. Fern tried to push it away with her mind.

"Ma'am, you need to wake up. Come on now, you'll be alright."

Her eyes fluttered open.

She stared up into a man's concern-filled gray eyes. His skin was tan and light brown hair curled down around his ears from under his hat. A smile quirked up under his equally curly, well-trimmed beard.

"Hey," he breathed. "You took a nasty spill there."

Her gaze darted to the side. The road was nearby, though she'd been moved off the rocks and something soft had been slipped beneath her shoulders and head. A bug crawled on her leg, and she idly thought about slapping it away, but her arm was heavy as a leaden post.

"Carl. The bees." She struggled to sit up.

"Don't be moving." The man laid a gentle hand on her shoulder. "I sent Jerry to find a doctor. My other worker is up the hill a ways. Your man is alive, but a little worse off than you, I'm afraid."

"Oh no. Poor Carl. I hope he's alright." She blinked, trying to clear the spots that danced before her eyes. "What about my wagon?"

He chuckled. "Showed up at the gates of our farm. That's what brought us here. One of your horses broke from the traces. We're not sure where it went, but the one mare is cool as cucumber sandwiches. All lathered up from the run though."

"And the bees?"

He pushed back his hat. "You and my bee-crazy father will be happy to know that the five buzzing boxes in the back of the wagon are unharmed. No cracks or breaks in the boards, which is lucky for the men who reached the wagon ahead of me."

She let out a shuddering sigh. "I'm glad the bees are safe. And your men. Hopefully, we can find the other horse before he hurts himself."

The man's forehead creased. "The most important thing is getting you and your fella to a place where you can rest."

He held out his calloused hand, stared at it, then shoved it into his pocket. "I'm Lawson Burke. Most folks call me Law. And I'm guessing you're the bee folks who were coming to teach my father how to keep 'em." He gave her an appraising look. "Though I didn't realize a woman was coming along."

"Nice to meet you, Law," she murmured. "I'm Fern Founder."

"Likewise," said Law. He started. "What am I thinking? You must be parched as August." He loosened a canteen from his belt and held it to her lips.

She raised her hand to steady the canteen. That's when she

realized some sort of cloth was pressed to her head. She touched it as she guzzled the cool liquid.

"Yes, you took a bit of a blow," Law said as he recapped the canteen. "But we stopped the bleeding. Didn't look too deep. Does it hurt much?"

She shook her head, but the movement sent fresh waves of pain tearing through her skin. "A little," she admitted.

He frowned and straightened, shielding his eyes as he gazed down the road. "Jerry should return shortly. I told him to send Father for the doctor and then bring a wagon so we could get you two back to the house and out of this sun. Then we'll take care of the bees, of course, though I'm not sure how to get them to their new home without starting a swarm."

As he spoke, the rattling of wheels sounded over the road.

"There he is," said Law. "Like a thunderbolt he falls."

This last sentence was murmured so quietly, Fern almost wondered if she'd imagined it. Strange that a work-hardened rancher would quote Tennyson. *I must be conjuring it up from somewhere in my blow-addled brain.*

Fern lowered her head and closed her eyes as the murmuring voices of two men filled her ears. Attempting to make out words proved to be too much effort, so she allowed the ebb and flow of conversation to soothe her into a drowsing haze.

Gentle arms lifted her body and laid her to rest on a soft surface. Wagon jolts sent pain into her head again. She bit her lip to keep from crying out.

An acrid, metallic stench of blood, one all too familiar from a lifetime of farm work, crept into her senses.

She turned her head, though the movement sent pain screaming through her body. Through slitted eyelids, she made out the blood-streaked face of Carl where he'd been placed beside her in the wagon.

"Carl," she whispered.

He didn't open his eyes.

A chill trickled down her spine. *What if he's dead?* Words bubbled up inside her but couldn't get past the bone-dryness of her throat, so she closed her eyes again.

After what seemed like an eternity, the movement finally stopped.

Boots crunched on rocks. "How are we doing?" asked Law.

"Is Carl–is he . . ."

"I don't know," he said softly. "He's breathing. The doctor will let us know, but his leg looks bad. We'll get your husband out first. Then we'll come back for you," he said in a gentle voice. "Will you be alright for a few minutes?"

"Yes," she said. "But he . . . Carl isn't my husband. He's our farmhand."

"Oh?" Law's eyebrow arched up to his hat. "My mistake. We'll be back for you in a jiffy."

Men surrounded the wagon. They talked and barked orders as they decided how to move Carl. The blankets beside her rustled, and he was lifted away from the wagon.

Then silence. She opened her eyes. Puffy clouds, the same ones they'd watched as they ate their lunch a few hours before, drifted over her head. Birds called to each other as they would on any other day.

A door slammed, and Law's face appeared once more. "All right, it's your turn now, Miss Founder." He tilted his head to the side. "It's proper to call you Miss Founder, I suppose, but you are such a Fern. I've never known a name to suit anyone so well in all my life."

Fern's lips twitched up at the corners. "That's fine with me."

"Glad we have that settled. Are you ready to be carried inside, oh fernest of Ferns?"

She braced herself against the wagon bed, but the moment she sat upright, her head started spinning. "Maybe if I rest here a short time, I can make it on my own."

"Nonsense. We don't want that head wound bleeding again. Allow me."

Before she knew it, powerful arms surrounded her, and her own hands were clasped around Law's broad shoulders. Her heart thudded against his chest. She hadn't been held this way since she was a little girl, by her father.

"There we are, hold tight." Law's voice trembled slightly,

whether from the effort of carrying her or something else, she didn't know.

When she attempted to hold up her head, dizziness came in a wave. She leaned her cheek against his rough shirt and closed her eyes. The aroma of hay and sunshine filled her senses.

"Hey, Frank, get that door for me," Law said.

Floorboards creaked under his boots, and the blurry images of walls and furniture shone through her slitted eyelids.

"Oh, dearie me," came a woman's voice. "Better put her in the second spare room. The man is already taking up the bed in the first one." The woman made a tsking noise. "I hope the doctor gets here soon, neither of them look too good."

Softness. Rest. The scent of lavender and rose enveloped her.

Law chuckled softly. "You can let go of me now."

Fern released her hold and fell back on a feather pillow. Relief flooded her soul, now she could settle and rest. Suddenly she very much wanted her mother and sisters. A tear burnt the corner of her eye.

"Now all you men leave the room." The woman's voice floated through the air. "I'll take care of Miss Founder until the doctor arrives."

Boots clomped away, and the door closed softly.

"I'm going to take off your shoes, dearie," said the woman's voice. "My name is Mrs. Crenshaw, and I'm the housekeeper.

Been here since Law was a boy."

"You . . . don't have to . . ." Fern tried to insist.

"No, no. Let me tend to you." While Mrs. Crenshaw talked, Fern felt her shoes and stockings being removed. Water dripped from somewhere, and then a deliciously cool wet cloth touched her forehead.

"I'll clean your wound; that way the doctor can see the scope of the problem immediately when he comes."

Fern winced and opened her eyes. A woman with a flat, doughy face and a housekeeper's bonnet peered at her through tiny spectacles.

The woman stepped back. "It's not that bad, Child. You'll be fine. Head wounds always bleed like a stuck pig, but 'tisn't deep. You're probably just weak from fright and blood loss. I'm afraid your dress is covered in blood and dirt and ripped beyond repair."

"Oh dear," said Fern. "My spare clothes are in the wagon."

"Don't worry about that now. I'll get you cleaned up and you can rest in your chemise. We'll tuck you up in this quilt when the doctor comes so nothing indecent peeps out."

"Alright." Fern would have agreed to dressing in a gunny sack at that point. Fatigue made her eyelids heavy. She drifted off to sleep, to the slosh of water in the basin and Mrs. Crenshaw's humming as she bustled about her work.

3

Heedless Choice

Fern awoke to the hearty call of a rooster outside her window.

Plumpett sounds different today. She pushed up on one elbow, intending to investigate, but her arm collapsed, and she sank back to the bed. "Ohhh," she groaned. Hints of dawn peeked through the curtains, revealing unfamiliar shapes and shadows. Pain pricked into her scalp as the previous day's events flooded back.

The door swung open, and Mrs. Crenshaw peeked in. "Good, good, you're awake! Hang on." A few moments later, she entered the room, balancing a tray. "I've brought you a morsel of breakfast. The doctor said you should eat a few bites as soon as you woke. How does ham and grits with biscuits sound?"

The tantalizing aroma of butter swirled from the loaded plate and Fern's stomach grumbled. "Wonderful."

Mrs. Crenshaw sat the tray on a little table. "Let me help you sit up." She adjusted the pillows behind Fern.

Fern bit her lip, trying not to wince at the movement.

"Oh, Dearie, I'm sorry, I know it hurts." Mrs. Crenshaw set the tray in Fern's lap. "Once you get some good food in you, I bet you'll feel better."

Fern stared down at the delicious-looking breakfast, arranged on delicate China. "Thank you. But what about Carl? And the bees? They're not still in the wagon, are they?"

Mrs. Crenshaw gave a short laugh. "Don't you worry about your little flying bugs. Mr. Burke cleared a nice patch under some trees in the orchard, and he's been fussing over them all morning. He would've hired maidens with palm fronds to fan them if he'd had the option."

"And Carl?"

The woman frowned. "Doc said he broke his leg in two places. The menfolks had a time setting it, but mercifully, Carl passed out in the middle. Doc said he'll heal, but it's gonna take a while."

"Oh. poor Carl."

"Poor both of you." Mrs. Crenshaw put a hand on her hip. "Doc said to watch you like a chicken on a grasshopper. Supposed to check your eyes to make sure you don't start looking in two directions at once." She peered into Fern's face, as though she expected this to happen at any moment.

"That would definitely be concerning." Fern picked up a biscuit, savoring the still-warm softness. "What about my mother? Can we send word to her? I doubt Carl will be able to travel for ages. They'll worry if we're not back in two weeks like we're supposed to be."

Mrs. Crenshaw pursed her lips. "Mr. Burke will figure something out. You're right, of course. We wouldn't want your mother to worry about you." She gave Fern a slanted look. "There isn't a Mister, is there?"

Fern blinked as she realized the woman was referring to herself and not her mother. "No, neither of us is married, actually. My mother is a widow and I'm an old maid."

Mrs. Crenshaw burst into a fit of snorting, spluttering laughter that could only be described as a mixture between a turkey gobbling and flies buzzing. She wiped her eyes with her apron. "Oh dear, such a young and beautiful girl calling herself an old maid. That's the silliest thing I've ever heard."

"Emerald City folks must look at the world differently than the good people of Cottage Grove." Fern finished the last of her biscuit and poured a little milk into her bowl of grits.

Mrs. Crenshaw tilted her head. "Maybe not them. But I do." She gestured to the small table. "Put your breakfast things there when you're finished, dear. I'll come back to check on you by and by."

Fern made quick work of the delicious food, though she missed the honey she normally put in her grits. *Soon this house will have some.* More than anything, she wanted to get out of bed and go check on her bees. *Ugh.* The drumming in her skull reminded her of the need to rest and heal.

Boots scraped the floor outside and someone rapped on the

bedroom door.

Fern shoved the tray to the side and pulled the covers up over the skimpy undergarments she still had on from the day before. *I must smell a fright.* "Come in," she said, as primly as she could muster.

Law Burke walked through the door, running a hand through his now hatless curls.

"Hello, ma'am. Fern." His broad shoulders filled the door frame, and he stood awkwardly, as though a beast not accustomed to being indoors. "Wanted to check on you. Mrs. Crenshaw said you're doing better today."

"I think I'll survive." Fern suddenly wished very much for a looking glass. "I can't thank you enough for rescuing us yesterday."

"Prettiest girl I've had the pleasure of rescuing." Law folded himself into the chair beside the bed.

"Am I the only girl you've ever rescued?" Fern asked in a teasing tone.

"Well now, Miss Fern, I am hurt beyond measure." Law's eyebrows knitted together, but he grinned broadly. "I might've had a few heroic moments in my life, but they're not worth speaking of."

"Mrs. Crenshaw said my bees were all right."

"Father has them settled; don't you worry about that. He's been talking about those bees for the last six months. Wanted them for years, you know. Thought about importing them from

California, but when he found a jar of your honey at a local market, he was delighted. We haven't moved 'em from the boxes yet, due to doctors and broken legs and injured maidens. But they're in a good spot."

"Are you interested in bees?" asked Fern.

"Not particularly." Law rubbed his beard, and his eyes brightened. "Of course, I didn't realize we'd have such a lovely beekeeper coming. If you're out there tending the creatures, I might take on a sudden interest." He tilted back his head.

"And I laugh to see them whirl and flee,
like a swarm of golden bees."

Shelly. I wasn't imagining it. He IS *quoting poetry!* Fern was used to all types of flirting, even had a few bad verses composed in her honor, but she'd dealt with them for so long that every compliment fell flat, like a bird smacking a glass windowpane. But Law was different. He gave his sentiments in such sweet, yet unabashed ways, they were almost endearing. *Not to mention he's ridiculously handsome.* But she'd encountered handsome before, and in the end, each suiter had been lacking. Certainly, she'd never found someone worth leaving home and sisters for.

Law rested his hands on his knees. "Say, you look tired, and the doctor said you should stay in bed at least one more day. Hopefully you'll be up and about tomorrow. Might even be able to visit your bees in person." He held up a palm. "Not that I'm rushing you any. I want to see you better, that's all."

"You're very kind." Fern picked crumbs from among the bedsheets and put them on the plate beside her.

"Are you finished there? Let me take all these things for you." Law whisked the tray from the bedside. "Now you can settle back and get some rest."

I'd love to find something to do. Fern had always been a restless soul and hated idle hands. With the pain in her head, reading didn't seem to be the best idea, though colorful books with tantalizing titles were lined up on the shelf across from her bed.

Perhaps Mrs. Crenshaw can drum me up some socks to mend. With all these men in the house, I bet there's a holey pile somewhere.

With that, she settled back in her bed. The last thought she had before drifting off again was a prayer. *Please God, help us figure out how to get word to Mother and my sisters. Help Carl mend quickly. And keep my bees safe.*

Iris drew the last frame from the hive and held it up, allowing the sunlight to filter through the golden combs. The gentle fragrance of wax and honey filled her senses. It was the most comforting scent a body could imagine.

There she is. The unmistakable long abdomen and dark coloration of the queen. The winged creature hid beneath the bodies of her swarming attendants.

Iris's lips curled into a smile. The queens this year were the nicest ones their apiary had seen. As far as she could tell, there would be twice as many workers than a usual yield, which was the reason they could afford to sell so many hives. *This honey season should be brilliant.*

She carefully replaced the frame and stepped back.

Time to go. Reluctantly, she gathered supplies in her basket and grasped the handle. Cricket chirps swelled, along with the sounds of early cicadas. Mother or Peony would be calling her for supper soon.

A safe distance from the hive, she removed her netted hat, the only protection she wore from her buzzing pets. After years of working with the bees, they'd come to an understanding, and she walked among them without fear.

A sudden sense of dread caused her to miss a step. Darkness filled her mind like drops of blood in water, swirling around dim shapes and faces.

A picture of her sister, still and bleeding, flickered into her mind. *Fern is hurt.* She sank to the ground. *Fern is hurt.*

After years of such premonitions, she knew better than to ignore the sensation. Leaning on a fallen log, she closed her eyes and focused. *Holy Spirit, what are you telling me? What should I do?*

Listen and pray. The quiet voice of her Father God spoke clearly, in the tone she knew so well. Though urgent, the voice brought a simple, immediate peace.

Iris rose from her makeshift seat and flew down the path toward the house, her basket banging from side to side. Instead of placing the items carefully in her 'bee cupboard' as she called the tiny shed off the side of the steps, she dumped everything on the porch and rushed through the kitchen door, not bothering to wash up or remove her shoes.

Myrtle stood by the kitchen's entrance. "Iris, what on earth! I was about to call you in for dinner."

Mother came in from the dining room. "Is everything alright? Were you stung?"

"N–no," Iris gasped. She placed a hand over her heaving chest. 'I–had a vision."

Peony came in to join them. "What happened?"

"It's Fern. And maybe Carl." Iris pulled off her thick leather gloves and sat to remove her shoes. "I believe they're in danger."

The color drained from Mother's face. The first few times Iris had shared her visions as a little girl, she'd laid them aside as childish fancy, but over the years, as they'd proven to be accurate, she'd given them proper credence.

"Should we send Richard after them?" Mother sank down in an overstuffed chair beside the door.

"The men are gone for the evening and won't return until Monday. They all live over an hour's ride away, and even if we go there, there's no telling if anyone will be home." Peony wiped her hands on her apron. "I don't know what we can do."

"Maybe we can pay someone from town to go," Myrtle suggested. "I'll ride in tomorrow and check with the sheriff."

"What will we tell them?" Iris groaned. "That I've had a vision from God? We all know how most folks would react."

Mother covered her face with her hands. "I've always allowed you girls to do as you wish. You've figured out troubles with courage and grace. Maybe this time I've gone too far. I shouldn't have let Fern go."

Peony perched on the arm of the chair and smoothed sweaty strands of hair back from Mother's face. "Don't worry, how could you have known? Fern is in God's hands. If she needs saving, he'll send angels."

"Maybe I could . . ." Iris began.

Mother held up a finger. "Don't say it, Iris. I'm not letting another one of you out of my sight, especially without an escort."

Iris pressed her arms against her chest, unspoken protests boiling over her tongue. Out of all the sisters, she and Fern were the closest. *I should've gone with her in the first place.* She'd felt that insistent nudging from the Holy Spirit when her mother had brought up the trip. She bowed her head. *Father, I'm sorry for not obeying you from the beginning.*

Later, Iris trembled beneath her quilt. The soft breathing of Peony and Myrtle rose and fell from the cots on either side of her, and a rare whippoorwill called from the giant cedar tree outside. The image of her sister, motionless and covered with blood, flashed in her mind whenever she closed her eyes. She longed for sleep, for some kind of escape from the scene, but it wouldn't go away.

Finally, she rose and dressed quickly in the thin slats of moonlight that shone through the tiny windows of the loft. Her sisters did not stir.

Once downstairs, she checked the clock. *Three.* Granny would be up in an hour. The old woman had never been able to break the habit of rising early. As the child of a sharecropper, she'd walked an hour each morning to work in a field all day.

Iris crept into the kitchen. She grabbed carrots, bread, and a small jar of honey, and stuffed everything into a flour sack.

Pausing by the third cupboard, she opened it slowly so it wouldn't creak. She fumbled through odds and ends until her fingers closed around a jar. She drew it out and studied the silver and gold coins, gleaming in the dim light. Mother never minded when they took what they needed, when they asked.

I'll have to beg for forgiveness instead of asking permission this time. Iris dropped five dimes into the reticule she always kept by her side. They clinked against her hand-pistol in a comforting way.

She pulled on her thickest boots and sunbonnet. Habit caused her to check the little mirror hanging in the kitchen alcove.

What am I thinking? Her mind raced. *I can't waltz down to*

Emerald City like this. She pulled the mirror from the wall and took it outside.

Thick dew instantly coated her shoulders and the top of her head. When she ran her hand over her hair, it came back wet. The three-quarter moon spilled light over the yard like an overturned milk barrel. *Glad I don't need a lantern.*

When she passed the chicken coop, Plumpett darted out and stared at her with a beady eye.

"You silly bird, it isn't nearly time to crow," she told him. He watched after her, but thankfully didn't make a sound.

In the barn, the cows lowed sleepy greetings, no doubt wondering why she was there to milk them two hours early.

"Go back to sleep," she hissed.

On the wall by the door hung several pairs of thick canvas coveralls she and her sisters wore for particularly nasty chores.

"These will have to do." She sighed and removed her dress and petticoats, glad none of the farm hands were around to burst in on her impromptu costume change. Bundling up the discarded clothes, she tossed them in her flour sack with the food. A plain cotton shirt paired well with the coveralls, and she topped everything off with a battered, floppy hat. Thankfully, the crown was tall enough to hold the pile of hair she tucked into it.

On her way to the stable, she caught up a piece of charcoal from the firepit where they burned brush. The charred stick chilled her skin as she rubbed it up and down her chin and over her upper lip.

She checked the mirror.

"Well, Iris, if no one looks too close, you could pass for a respectable man."

Her horse nickered while she saddled her up and filled a small bag with oats. "Hope you're rested, Shae. We're off on an adventure."

As she grabbed the saddle horn and prepared to mount, she glanced back at the house.

I didn't write a note. They'll be beside themselves. Mother would need time, but she was more than accustomed to Iris making impulsive decisions.

No time to sneak back in for pen and paper. She grabbed the last bit of charcoal and scrawled a note on a flat piece of scrap wood. Stealing back into the barn, she left it, along with the mirror, next to the milking pail, where Peony would arrive in a short while.

Stepping back out, she stared up at the pale moon, which still shone in the early morning shadows.

God, please keep me safe. The certainty of her decision made her light, giddy almost. The fear of facing countless unknown strangers was tempered by the excitement of a daring adventure to new places. This struggle was familiar, one she always experienced before a change. *Please let Fern be safe.*

In moments she was astride her mare, thundering down the driveway in the direction of the fabled coast . . . and hopefully her sister.

ANGELA CASTILLO

4
Honey and Sunshine

Iris slumped in the saddle. Every muscle ached, and her belly grumbled. She had only paused once to polish off the rest of her food, preferring to avoid cities and squinting stares from inquisitive townspeople.

"Whoa there, Shae." Iris paused in a patch of waning sunlight. The mare was a dandy one, and had seen Iris through mud and snow, but her hooves clomped against the packed earthen road in a half-hearted canter and she flattened her ears against her head.

As they stopped, Iris drew a map from her pocket. She unfolded it and studied the hand-drawn lines, almost impossible to see for the creases.

Fern and Carl had planned to stay in the next town over for their second night of travel. *Do I ride in and ask if they came through? What if they never reached it? Surely I would have found signs of the wagon. Unless someone stole it.* A chilly ache settled between her shoulder blades.

The sun dipped dangerously low into the trees. *I must stop for the night.* Even with the full moon, this road was no place for a lone evening traveler.

She pulled her hat down low and clicked to Shae. Fern was the one who'd always done well in the little school plays and pageants; Iris was hard-pressed to be someone besides herself. She'd never cared for acting, and she didn't relish the idea now. Hopefully, no one would expect her to engage in conversation. She'd simply find the boardinghouse, make her inquiry, and rent a room for the night. With any luck they'd have a private room to spare. Sometimes boarding houses were so busy that they'd only have crowded bunkhouses for men to sleep in.

In the last town, she'd met more than one suspicious stare, mostly from the matronly, middle-aged women with enormous hats. *I must add a swagger to my step.* She toyed with finding a chaw of tobacco somehow, but the smell alone made her nauseous.

A sign announced the town was a quarter of a mile away. "Almost there," she promised Shae.

Firelight glowed through a grove of lanky saplings. Men's voices drifted through the trees. A barking laugh rang out, accompanied by snatches of song.

The hairs on the back of her neck stood on end, and dread pooled over her soul like a thundercloud. She pressed tightly to Shae's back and held her breath, though the chance of being heard through the racket was slim.

"Hey, Mister. Got a nickel?"

Iris bit back a scream, while Shae jolted and tensed.

A scrawny piebald with a hulking rider blocked her way.

The powerful stench coming from their general vicinity slammed her in full force, though she couldn't tell if the origin was from man or beast. The man's shirt was mostly patches, and his ragged beard was dotted with chunks of food.

Her mind raced. The reticule held a handkerchief and three remaining dimes. If she tried to give this man anything, she had a terrible feeling he would take all she had and perhaps kill her as well. *Or worse.* She did have her small pistol, but it was out of reach in her saddlebags, with no hope of grabbing it in time. The last thing she needed was a gun duel on the darkened road.

Fear crawled over her skin like a frenzied spider. "I have nothing for you," she said in the deepest tones she could muster.

"Bad decision, Mister." The last rays of the ebbing sun caught the glint of a rifle as the man leveled it at her head.

Iris leaned far over Shae's side and dug her heels into the mare's ribs. "Hey there! Girl, get on!" she screamed.

Shae bolted forward as the rifle cracked its report.

A bullet whizzed by Iris's head as she righted herself, clutching handfuls of mane and reins.

The man bellowed behind her, and another man answered. Hooves pounded the road.

"Go, girl," she pleaded in Shae's ear. "You're faster than that nasty horse!"

Shae stretched out over the dirt road as though the very Devil were behind them, as surely he was.

Welcoming lights from farmhouses shone like beacons, dotting the hills.

If I can only reach town. Please, God, let me reach town.

Another twist and turn, and the road opened wide and straight. She sat up in the saddle. "Woah, Girl. Calm down. We're safe now."

Shae slowed to a trot, lather bubbling on her neck. She shook her head.

"Good girl. That's a lady." Iris slid from the saddle, drenched with sweat. Tears poured down her cheeks, and her chest ached as she struggled for breath. "There's a good girl," she whispered to Shae.

Gathering every ounce of courage, she craned her neck to check the road. *No one.* Fear bounced off her shoulders, replaced by indescribable relief.

As much as she'd hoped to not bring attention to herself, she'd be forced to report the strange men. Surely the law enforcement responsible for this area would want to know of the danger.

I'd better fix my whiskers first. Ducking her head, she prayed the streets would remain quiet as she led her horse past the buildings in search of the inn.

###

Tom nudged his velvety nose against Fern's shoulder, begging for more of the carrot slivers she kept in her pocket.

"You shouldn't get any treats after the way you behaved the other day," she scolded. "We're lucky that farmer found you and brought you back."

The hayloft loomed above her, stuffed with a season's worth of bales. The other horses in the stalls poked their heads out, hoping for their own share of carrots. All were sturdy quarter horses, since the two hundred head of cattle must be wrangled. The thought of caring for all those breathing creatures made Fern dizzy. Bees were much better. Yes, they could fly away, and sometimes stings were unavoidable, but usually they stayed in the small boxes and behaved themselves.

Mrs. Crenshaw had fussed and fidgeted when Fern begged to get out of bed, but she'd insisted. Two days was long enough, and her head had stopped throbbing for the most part. Fern's need to check on her beasts and desire to see the ranch won over any lingering pain.

Law came to the barn's entry and leaned against the frame.

When their eyes met, Fern's breath caught in her throat. Sudden heat crept to her cheeks, making her wish the place wasn't so stuffy. She drifted to the barn's window, hoping her discomfort wasn't obvious.

"Good morning," Law said. "You must be feeling better today."

Fern slipped the last of her carrots to Tom and wiped her

hands on her pinafore. "I am, thank you. Much better."

"I'm so glad." He gave her a warm smile. "And Carl is on the mend as well?"

"Yes, I visited him earlier. He's suffered much pain, but the doctor said he should mend if there's no mortification. At least the bones broke cleanly." She smoothed Tom's mane against his broad neck, working out the tangles and burrs with her fingers. "I'm sorry we'll be forced to beg hospitality for longer than planned, but the doctor says it might be a month before Carl can take the journey home." The thought of being away from her family for such a long time gave her a hollow feeling in the pit of her stomach.

Law nodded, his eyebrow arching. "I'm delighted you'll be here longer, and I think Mrs. Crenshaw will feel the same. I'm sure she gets lonely sometimes, as the only woman in the household." He tilted his head. "She's been with us for seventeen years, ever since my mother died."

"I'm sorry she's gone. My father also passed when I was young, at five years old on the Oregon trail."

Law's eyes narrowed.

"When I come to the end of the road," he murmured

"And the sun has set for me
I want no rites in a gloom filled room
Why cry for a soul set free?"

"I don't recognize that one," Fern said.

"Christina Rossetti." He blinked. "*Let Me Go*. They read it at her funeral. Mother was such a young thing, Father always says. Twenty-six when she passed. We lived in a little cottage in the back." He pointed south, to a patch of woods that stood out like a darkened paintbrush against the expanse of pasture. "After she died, we moved to Grandfather's house. Father never went to our little home again."

"And he didn't remarry?" Fern asked.

"Nope." Law straightened and walked over to Tom. "Anyway, I came to fetch you, if you'll come. Father wanted to discuss the bees with you, since your farm hand is poorly and you'd probably know more about them anyway. I'm no help. I'm more of a cattle man, myself."

"Oh, bees aren't for everyone." Fern followed Law as he headed back down a twisty path she hadn't taken yet. "Do you know they can sense fear? One reason we wear netted hats. If a person screams or shouts near the hive, the swarm might fly right down their throat. It happened to one of our farm hands." To Fern's satisfaction, Law's eyes grew bigger as she continued. "Fortunately, only one bee made it down. His tongue swelled up so big he couldn't speak for three days. Grandma said it was a blessing in disguise since the ranch hand had given us other trouble. Mother said she was being uncharitable."

"Mercy." Law drew his hat down over his face. "As much as it pains me to lose your company, I believe I'll stay back here and muck out a few stalls." He pointed through the trees. "Father's right down there, if you keep following the path."

"If you're certain you don't want to join me." Fern was tempted to laugh at the thought of the tall, muscular man being afraid of tiny winged insects, but she'd seen the same fear in burlier men's eyes.

Law bowed his head. "I'll visit them another day. When I have a netted hat." He touched her hand. "Until then, *'though your parting dims the day,'* I will endure."

More poetry. Fern shook her head as she hurried down the path. Law certainly was charming, with his quotes and the tender concern he held for her. *I've heard sweet words before.* Though her mind gave her this gentle reminder, her heart melted a teensy bit more, like warm honey in the golden sunshine.

Twigs snapped beneath her feet as the trees thinned.

Mr. Burke, the owner of the ranch, beamed at her through his netted veil. He'd stuffed his gray beard up under the fabric, and his brown eyes twinkled beneath his hat's wide brim. His short, stout figure was dwarfed by his son when the two stood together.

Fern had encountered him only twice, the first while she was still in bed. He'd been so persistent with questions about the bees that Law had insisted he leave the room so she could have peace.

"I've placed the boxes yonder." He waved to a stack of crates under the shady trees. "I want to move them to their hives today. Do you think that would be good?"

His voice sounded so anxious Fern was tempted to pat him on

the shoulder.

She examined the wooden boxes he'd prepared for hives. She counted five, one for each box they'd brought. Each one was about thirty inches high, thirty inches wide, and twelve inches deep. She opened a door in the front to reveal rows of tiny drawers that slid out as small flat trays.

"I've never seen hives like this," she said.

"They're the latest thing," said Mr. Burke. "I ordered them specially from California." He raised a bushy eyebrow beneath his veil. "Do you think they'll work?"

"I don't see why not; they seem roomy enough." Fern replaced the drawer. "But you never know with bees."

Mr. Burke led her to the stack of small boxes holding the colonies. "We removed the stoppers, so they've been free to come and go. The little darlings made quick work getting to that field of wildflowers I fenced off from the cows and horses." He swept out his arm. "Field's full of rabbit holes anyway."

Fern studied the expanse of gold, blue, and purple blooms that nodded in the sunlight.

"Those will do nicely, Mr. Burke. And the crops of the nearby farmers will thank you as well, once you build up your hives."

Mr. Burke smiled. "Ain't that pollination amazing? I suspect I'll have a line of buyers to the next county, providing I cultivate enough hives to spare some for my neighbors."

"Chances are good," replied Fern. "And I see you've set out the supplies I brought."

"Yes." Mr. Burke pried off the lid of the small box and set it aside. His hands shook ever so slightly.

"Mr. Burke, no need to be nervous. We need to keep calm around the bees, with no sudden movements, and all will be well."

Mr. Burke glanced up. "Oh, I'm not worried about being stung. I'm just so excited." He lowered his voice to a whisper. "I might jump right out of my skin!"

"Let me show you how handle this," said Fern. "Steel nerves make sweet bees, my sister Iris says."

One by one, they pried the lids off the wooden crates and poured the boxes of bees into their new homes in brown and gold cascades.

Fern found conversation flowed easily with Mr. Burke. They chatted about her best honey harvests and the challenges they'd faced at the Founder farm.

After a while, Mr. Burke squinted up at the sun. "Best get back to the house. Mrs. Crenshaw doesn't appreciate when we let her vittles get cold."

"She cooks food for everyone *and* runs the household?" asked Fern as they walked back.

Mr. Burke removed his veil and hat and ran his fingers through a mop of gray hair. "Yes, bless her soul. Of course, us menfolk try to clean up after ourselves in a fashion. She scrubs that floor so hard you'd think there'd be a hole to China by now."

Law sauntered up to them as they approached the house. "Hey there, good to see the bees didn't carry you away. Miss Fern, I keep forgetting to tell you. Your mare threw a shoe when she spooked the other day."

"Oh." Fern pulled off her veil and hat, thankful she'd plaited her hair back tight against her head. "I'm glad my horses weren't lamed to ruin with the condition of that road." She wrinkled her nose. "I suppose I'll have to get Sue reshod before we take the wagon back home." Though Fern liked horses just fine, Iris was really the horsewoman of the family.

"Certainly." Law rubbed the back of his neck. "I can take her to the farrier after lunch. If you feel up to it, I'd be honored for you to accompany me."

"I bet you would," snorted Mr. Burke. He gave Fern a mischievous grin.

Law rolled his eyes. "Shall we venture to lunch, m'lady?" he asked Fern, holding out his elbow.

"We shall." Fern folded her fingers over the offered arm. His gallant ways were over the top, but for some reason she found herself looking forward to each silly gesture.

In the dining room, the wooden table, fashioned from long planks of yellow pine, shone in the brilliant sunlight pouring in from tall picture windows. Paintings of long-gone family members stared down from an assortment of frames, interspersed with mounted deer antlers and cow horns.

Before they sat down, Law gestured to four men Fern hadn't met, who were now gathered around the table. "Fern, meet Hank and George. Richard and Jerry helped rescue you a few days ago."

"Nice to meet you." Fern nodded to each of them. "Thank you so much for your help."

"Weren't nothin', Ma'am," said Jerry.

Mr. Burke led Fern to the head of the table, while he took a chair to the side. She suspected this was intended to keep her from the men's jostling ways as they passed stacks of fried chicken and steaming piles of corn bread. Now and then, when one of them committed a particularly unpleasant vulgarity, Law would give them a glare and they'd mutter an apology.

Fern, being used to such mannerisms with the farmhands who crowded their porch at harvest time, ignored these breaches of etiquette and ate her lunch with gusto. Mrs. Crenshaw beamed at her from the other end of the table.

"Your cornbread is so crisp and delicious," Fern said to Mrs. Crenshaw. "I must get your recipe for my sisters."

Two bright pink spots rose on Mrs. Crenshaw's cheeks. "Thank you, dearie. Carl seemed to like it especially. He wanted to join us, but it still hurts for him to move."

"Thank you for caring for him," said Fern. I hope he feels better soon."

"I'm simply thankful you're both on the mend," Mrs. Crenshaw replied.

Fern munched her cornbread in silence. *It's a miracle we weren't killed. Somehow, we must get word to Mother.*

5

The Untamed Sea

Law swung open the large gate that closed off the Burke's farm from the rest of civilization. He gestured to Fern. "You can bring her on through."

Fern tugged on the giant horse's lead. "Come on, Sue. Let's get your shoe fixed."

Sue snorted and shook her mane, then stepped forward tentatively.

Law put his hands on his hips. "She sure is particular about her feet. It's funny about these big horses, isn't it? Hooves that could squash a rat, but if the tiniest thing bothers them, they act like princesses."

Fern laughed. "It's true. Especially Sue. You should see when she walks through the mud. She comes as close to tiptoeing as any horse could."

They'd only made it a short way down the road when Law slapped his forehead. "I forgot to tell Jerry to move the herd to the southern pasture. I'd better run and let him know. With any luck he's still in the barn. Mind waiting for me?"

Fern stared out at the never-ending fields and forests, filled with more textures and colors than a crazy quilt. "I'll be fine."

Law jumped the gate and disappeared.

Fern leaned against Sue's obliging back and smiled. She'd known this trip would change her soul, like the rich dyes changed ordinary cloth into fabrics fit for a king's court. But she hadn't counted on Law. Already the thought of parting from him wore on her mind. She patted her cheeks. *Plenty of time to worry about that later. Enjoy the day, Fern Founder.*

Hooves clopped from the hill, and a carriage rattled over the stones.

In Cottage Grove, there weren't too many of what Peony called "rich folks." Most people owned modest farms and sturdy, serviceable homes, with little to boast about. 'Well-off' meant you had plenty to eat and warm clothes for the winter.

In all her born days, Fern had never seen anything as fine as that carriage. The matched black horses had not a star or stocking to tell them apart. The polished sides of the coach gleamed in the sun, as though forbidding dust from the road to sully them. In the driver's seat, sitting straight as a fireplace poker, was the coachman, wearing a type of top hat Fern had only seen in fairytale illustrations.

A man called from inside the coach. "Woah, William. Stop here, would you?"

The horses came to a halt a few yards away from Fern. Sue sidled away from them; her ears flattened against her head.

Fern patted her nose. "Calm down, sweet girl. All is well." Her own throat was dry, and a thin stream of sweat trickled down her back.

The man peered out of the carriage. A shining hat also sat upon his head, though it was shorter and rounder than the coachman's. His face was clean-shaven, with piercing eyes set over an aristocratic nose and a rather pointed chin. If not for the cold, calculating air that hung over him, he would have been staggeringly handsome.

"How do you do?" said Fern, for it seemed the way to address such a person.

The man blinked. "I do? I'm doing well, thank you." He stepped from the carriage and held out a gloved hand. "Graham Timmis, at your service." A smooth scar, shaped like a half-moon, ran from the corner of his eye to his jawline.

Fern allowed him to squeeze her fingers, then pulled her hand back to hold Sue, who jerked her head up and danced in quick, impatient steps. "Fern Founder. Forgive me, my horse is unsettled."

"Oh." Graham squinted at Sue. "Fine animal." His tone indicated his feelings did not match the words. "Do you need assistance?"

"Kind of you to offer, Sir, but my help should return shortly. We're walking her to the farrier, whom I understand is not far down this road."

"'Tis so," said Graham. He gave her an appraising look, which rankled her, though she didn't know why. "You must be new to town. I've never had the pleasure of meeting you."

Fern dipped her head. "Yes, I'm staying at the Burke's farm, but I travelled from Cottage Grove. I'm from a family of beekeepers and I came to instruct Mr. Burke in the raising of his apiary."

"Bees? How fascinating!" Graham's mouth sagged at the corners. "But you didn't say you were staying with the Burkes, did you? Surely a different place?"

"Yes, the Burkes." She glanced back. *What is keeping Law?*

"Ah." He raised his eyebrows at the coach, and the man shrugged. "That is unfortunate."

Irritation bloomed within Fern. "They have been nothing but kind to me, Sir. I don't know what you could be implying."

All remaining pleasantness drained from Graham's face. "You're free to do as you please, my lady, but if you find yourself in need of anything, come to my estate. I live with my elderly aunt on the hill yonder in the white manor." He gestured down the road. "On the other side of the Burkes." He spoke the name with twisted lips, as though it came with a sour odor. "We raise the finest horses in the state of Oregon. You can count on my assistance if you feel any danger."

He climbed back into the carriage, tipped his hat, and the coachman drove on.

Fern crossed her arms and pressed them against her chest, quivering with indignation. *Who does that man think he is?*

Then another thought entered her mind. *What if Graham is right? I've only been here a few days, and don't know much about the Burkes.*

Law came back up the driveway, whistling. His cheerful face brought her a flood of reassurance. She remembered how tenderly he'd carried her into the house after the accident. *Pooh. This man couldn't possibly be the least bit dangerous.*

Law took Sue's reins. "And we're off to the farriers!" He glanced at her face, and his eyebrows drew together over his nose. "Is everything all right, oh fairest of the Ferns?"

She stared at her feet, watching clouds of dust puff around them as they walked. "I think so. I met one of your neighbors, Mr. Graham Timmis."

"Oh. Him," Law's voice was tight.

"Yes. He doesn't seem to like you very much." Fern instantly regretted the words. She had a terrible habit of inserting herself into other people's affairs, and this seemed like a matter she'd want to avoid like an angry skunk.

"You would be correct in that assumption," Law said. He gave her a quick, bright smile. "Whatever he told you, it happened many years ago, and based on hurts he's carried within him all this time. We both wronged each other. I've forgiven him, but he shall never forgive me, I'm afraid. Let's not spoil this beautiful day by discussing it further." He held out his arm in his normal, gallant fashion.

"Fine." Fern took his elbow. But she couldn't stuff down the curiosity that now burned in her heart.

###

After Sue was settled with the farrier, Law led Fern back down the road. "It'll be a few hours 'till Mr. Miller can get to Sue." He flashed her a grin. "Today's my day off. Father makes sure everyone gets a day's break during the week, in addition to a half-day on Sunday so we can all go to church. We can't skip everything on Sunday, or the cows would burst their udders." He reddened. "Sorry for the vulgar talk."

Fern chuckled. "Sounds like something my grandma would say. As someone who has milked cows most of my life, I'm not offended easily."

His eyes travelled slowly across her face. This scrutiny didn't make her angry, like it had with Mr. Timmis, but she couldn't help but pat her hair.

"You're so different, Fern. So strong and sure of yourself. I've never met anyone like you," Law said.

"And I've never met a rancher who quotes poetry," she said lightly, but her heart thudded against her chest so hard she was sure he could hear it.

"With a name like Law, you'd think my parents hoped I'd become a sheriff or a judge," he said. "But I've always loved the ranch. My father says I was out mucking stalls and following the cows around soon as I could walk."

"Well, I'm not much for growing plants," said Fern. "Though I do like to see new kinds of flowers and trees."

"Tell you what." Law drummed his fingers against his cheek. "Since I have the day off, would you like to see the ocean? I remember you saying you'd never been there, and the farrier offered to lend me his buggy. We're only a couple of miles away."

She clasped her hands together before her. "Would I! It's only been my dearest dream!"

Law lifted his hands. "Far be it from me to deny your dearest dream, my lady. But is your head all right?"

Fern touched the small bandage that still covered the wound. "I'll be fine."

The farrier's buggy was small and light, and it only took them a few moments to hitch up the roan mare he'd said they could borrow.

Law helped Fern into her seat and squeezed his tall, slender frame into the other side. "Tight but cozy, don't you think?"

Fern pulled off her straw hat and fanned herself with it. "Cozy is fine." Their shoulders brushed when she leaned against the thin cushion, and a slight tremor ran to her spine. *Did he notice? Would I mind if he did?*

Law slapped the reins against the carriage horse's gleaming

chestnut back and the animal ambled forward.

"Not quite as refined as the matched pair belonging to Graham Timmis," Law said.

Fern tipped her head. "She's well-cared for and loved, and that's what's important."

The wagon wheels clattered on the rocky road, which was much smoother than the perilous hill which had caused her and Carl so much trouble a few days before.

Fern's head throbbed slightly, and she blinked away the pain. *It will not happen again, and I won't be afraid. I'm going to enjoy my day.*

The sun beamed gently over the carriage. Fields and fields of flowers in every color flashed brightly, as though each attempted to outdo the last, like a lady's hat contest at a county fair.

"We'll take the road that edges around town." Law pointed to a side path that wound through a tunnel in the trees. "It's market day. Don't want to give the biddies reason to wag their tongues and we won't be able to fit through the carts and crowds anyway." He turned and smiled. "I'll take you into town another time, Is that all right? The docks are a mile past, and filled with rough, heathen sailors, so we probably we won't ever go there, unless you truly desire to see boats."

"I trust you, Law." Fern meant the words. Otherwise, how else would she be riding along on a secluded drive with a near stranger? This man gave her a homey feeling, like she'd always known him. She felt as safe as Grandma's new orange kitten, curled up with the giant retriever in front of the fire at home.

The carriage trundled left at a fork in the road, and they entered a dense forest. Instant coolness enveloped them, and Fern's ears became muffled, as though she'd wrapped a shawl around her head.

"We'll cut through the hills here," said Law. He sniffed the air. "If you pay attention, you can catch a hint of salt, even though the trees mask it in part."

Fern threw back her head and closed her eyes. The richness of the soil, the fresh green scent of the enormous cedars surrounding them . . . and there it was. A tang of salt, drifting in at the end of the other scents, popping in like a purple flower in a field of yellow. "It smells like an enchanted land," she said.

"It'll become stronger as we near the sea," said Law. He cupped his hand behind his ear. "And if you listen, you can hear the gulls."

Sure enough, the eerie cries sounded through the thicket, longing voices telling of fish, flight, and adventure.

The road wove in and out of the trees until they thinned once more. The light grew stronger. At last, the carriage broke through into streaming sunlight. Large boulders rose on either side of the road, and the grass grew higher, thicker. Sand dusted the path.

"And there's the sea." Law pulled back on the reins, and the horse slowed her step. "Right over this hill."

Fern stood in the buggy seat, clutching Law's shoulder for support. She gasped.

A wide expanse of bluish green stretched into a distance she couldn't fathom. Rocks in all sorts of strange shapes and sizes hugged the shore, while waves swirled and crashed around them, revealing their origins. These boulders differed from the stony edifices she vaguely remembered on the Oregon Trail. The ocean-formed stones shone, pounded by wind, salt, sand and sea spray.

"Don't fall out of the wagon again, remember what happened last time." Law chuckled. His hands tensed on the reins and the horse's ear flicked back. The mare stopped.

He drew up the leads and tied them to a sturdy sapling. "Jemima will be fine here while we explore."

Fern slipped out of the carriage before Law could come around to give her a hand. She hurried down the thin strip of bare earth that served as a pathway between a fringe of waving marsh grasses. As she passed, she broke off a stalk and examined it. This grass was thick and meaty, a different type than she'd seen in any prairie or field. *Curious how things can grow while being pelted by salty air.* But somehow it did, and thrived, for it grew everywhere.

The wind tugged at her sunbonnet, and she pulled the hat off her head, allowing it to dangle behind her back. Strands of hair whipped from her updo, blowing into her face. A section flew into her mouth, and she tasted salt.

"Wait up," Law said behind her. "The trail gets tricky here." His shadow loomed tall and dark beside hers on the path. "Not that you seem to be a woman who needs assistance."

"I don't," she replied, realizing how snobbish that sounded the moment she said it, but not quite regretting the words.

A broad grin spread over his face. "You might like it, sometime."

What could he possibly mean by that? She lifted her chin and continued down the path, towards the crashing waves.

The trail meandered along the bluff, steep but still manageable. Below them was a giant rock sculpture, with a window opening out into the sea. The sand below was undisturbed at first, shining like a polished tabletop. Then the water lapped over it like maple syrup, oozing over the sand, foaming on the edges, to be sucked away again into oblivion.

Fern sat on a rounded boulder and snatched off her boots and stockings, not caring when Law reddened and looked away. Mother had never been one to quibble about ankles, and her daughters often ran through the farm barefooted, no matter what company came to grace their table. Mother had been reprimanded once by the local minister, and she'd simply snapped that if God hadn't wanted girls to show their ankles, then he wouldn't have made summertime.

After discarding her footwear in an untidy heap, Fern hitched up her skirts and darted toward the water, avoiding the sharp little seashells dotting the ground.

When she first stepped into the sand, her feet sank in the sticky mess and soon her toes disappeared. But as she approached the lapping waves, the sand became firm, her soles barely making prints, until water foamed around her feet. She lifted her skirts out of reach from the waves and watched in fascination as her feet were swallowed in a sandy gulp.

Law came beside her, his feet also bare, his trousers rolled up to his knees.

"For I was as it were a child of thee,
And trusted to thy billows far and near,
And laid my hand upon thy mane—as I do here."

The corner of his mouth curled into a soft smile, and his eyes glistened. "Your happiness is a sight to behold." He pointed to a boulder. "This area is shallow. We should be able to wade out a bit and see beyond this rock."

"Ooh, lovely!" Fern said. "I'd love to explore a bit farther!" She pulled a foot from the sand's sucking grasp, then the next one.

"Stick to the edge." Law warned. "There's a drop off pretty close. I don't believe we're prepared for a full dunking. Our families might tolerate a quick visit to the shore, but your mother would probably have a fit of the vapors if we ended up going for a swim, no matter how unplanned."

Fern giggled. "I couldn't imagine my mother having a fit of any kind. I believe swimming is off the table, even though I know how. I would like to see beyond this rock."

Law held out an obliging elbow, and she grasped it, keeping hold of her skirts with her other hand. They sloshed through the ankle-deep water, sand sucking at their feet with every step.

At least a dozen blobby brown creatures the size of deer lounged on the rocks several yards away. Occasionally, one would break from the group and slide into the ocean.

"Are those sea lions?" Fern asked.

Law nodded. "I wish you could see the otters. You will never find a more playful creature. They're like puppies, the way they frolic in the waves. I don't see any today." He pointed to a group of funny little birds with orange beaks. "Those are puffins."

"They look like children's toys," said Fern.

She stared down into the gentle waves. Through clouds of sand, little fishes gleamed bright in the dappled sunshine. They swam around her toes, tickling her skin.

Law studied the fish–or perhaps her feet. "My mother loved it here. She'd watch the minnows, just like you."

"What happened to her, if you don't mind me asking?"

"Died in childbirth. Along with my baby sister." Pain flickered through Law's eyes. "She's the reason I love poetry. She quoted things all the time, and I inherited her poetry books when she passed. The sonatas and ballads comforted me in the following years, and I added to my collection every time I'd find another volume in the store."

"I'm so sorry," Fern murmured.

Law ran a hand over his face. "Yes. A child should never be forced to endure such a thing. So many do."

"Yes. I barely remember my father," said Fern.

A swollen wave swept up Fern's leg, and she yelped. "I'd

better return to dry land, or these skirts will stay sodden all day."

"Yes, we should make our way home before lunch," said Law, a touch of regret in his voice. "Mrs. Crenshaw will send the entire garrison of hired hands out after us if we don't."

As they slogged back to shore, he touched her shoulder. "I didn't mean to fill your outing with stories of sorrow. My father and I have come through the valley to a better place, with help from God Almighty. Though I believe my mother could have kept me from some of the reckless choices I made in my younger days."

Fern wondered if those bad choices were what Graham Timmis had alluded to. But it would be impolite to push the matter further, especially after Law had so tenderly opened his heart to her. After years of working with hardened, leathered farmhands, it was refreshing to have a sensitive man in her company. The only hints of sensitivity she usually saw in men (besides Carl, who couldn't kill a fly,) had been clumsy attempts at gentility from the parade of suitors who marched to their farm in attempts to woo a sister. Some of them came straight from the Oregon trail, in suits sharp with creases, looking for a ready-made homestead, with cooks and wives waiting for them. Iris called these "Box Badgers." If they arrived at the farm and were lucky enough to meet Mrs. Founder, Myrtle or Peony first, they might get a hot meal, or if nothing else, a handful of cookies before being sent on their way. However, unfortunate indeed was the man who encountered Iris on the driveway. If a fellow could not manage to stammer out a good enough explanation for his presence, he might be assaulted by several well–aimed dirt clods. Fern wasn't ashamed to say she had thrown her fair share.

Fern smiled at the memory, then glanced up to see Law staring at her, one eyebrow raised.

"Oh, sorry," she said. "Yes, of course we should go back. It's hard to leave now that I'm here. The place is even more beautiful and enthralling than I imagined." She bent down and chose a few small shells, wiping the sand from them with the corner of her apron. "These will be perfect for my sisters. And my mother will love them as well. She always read us fairy stories about the sea, and now there it is, right in front of me. These very water droplets connect to foreign soils I can only ever dream about."

Law guided her back up the path. "I never thought about it, but I suppose you're right." He handed her into the buggy and tilted his head. "How do you do that?"

"Do what?"

"Add a bit of magic to everything. You're like a poem wrapped in the skin of a beautiful woman."

For the first time in ages, her cheeks warmed, and she covered them with her hands. "Land sakes, Mr. Burke. You've made me blush like a child."

"That's exactly how you make me feel," said Law, as he climbed into the wagon and took hold of the reins. "Like a schoolboy."

6
Unexpected Dinner Party

Intense violet threads crept up through the vermillion sky, skirting the clouds in a foreboding tint. Iris scowled. Twilight was usually her favorite time of day, but now she wished for an hour more of daylight, perhaps two. Thankfully, a farmer she'd encountered had confirmed she'd almost arrived in Emerald City. But the woods seemed ever thicker, and since then she'd seen no house or farm or soul. A chill wind seeped through the coarse fabric of her button–up shirt. *Why didn't I bring warmer clothes?*

Besides the terrifying encounter with the ruffians of the previous evening, she'd had no problems. Her disguise, though hastily assembled, had worked well, with merely a tipped hat or two to acknowledge her presence. She'd even had last night's innkeeper offer her the hayloft for half price. He'd have never suggested such a thing if he'd known her true identity.

"I should travel like this more often," she said to her mare.

Shae flicked her grey-white ears back and snorted.

"I know, girl. You're ready for home and hay. Well, if you'd pick your feet up a bit and stop avoiding each little puddle in the road, we'd get there faster," Iris teased.

Shae's muscles tensed.

Clopping hooves and the jingle of a harness sounded on the road behind them.

Iris craned her neck for a better glimpse. "Another farmer? We'll pray he has good news."

But it wasn't a farmer. Instead, a brightly polished coach and gleaming stallions appeared around the bend. Iris's heart bounded. She always appreciated beautiful horses and had secretly dreamed of owning a matched pair someday. *But mine would be white, not black...*

"Sir!" a voice, firm but kind, rang through the woods. "How goes the journey?"

"It would go very well." Iris answered, trying to make her voice deep and rough as possible, and also stifling a giggle at her own efforts. "If I could find my intended destination before it grows too dark. I have no lantern and know nothing of this area."

The coach halted, and the carriage driver tipped his stove-pipe hat. A slender, gloved hand appeared at a little side window, and a woman peered out. Wrinkles covered rather flabby cheeks, and steel-gray curls tumbled from beneath her fashionable straw bonnet. "Sir, you look a bit puny to be out here on the road all by yourself, especially this late at night."

"Aunt Corianne!" a male voice from inside the buggy snapped. "You shouldn't speak to a fellow in that manner. You might embarrass him."

A man looked through the window, whilst the elderly woman retreated with a huff. "Pardon my aunt. We don't see too many strangers in these parts."

"I'm looking for a rancher by the name of Burke," said Iris.

The elderly woman's face popped back, and Iris really did stifle a laugh this time; she so resembled a chipmunk peering out of a burrow.

The woman pursed her wrinkled lips and gave a slight shake of her head.

The gentleman left the carriage through the door on the opposite side and walked around it. "My good fellow. I'm mystified that suddenly the road teems with those who desire to associate with the people the likes of the Burkes."

"Oh?" Iris fought to keep the surprise from her voice. "I take it you don't much care for the Burkes?"

The gentleman adjusted an already perfect cufflink. "Can't say they're my favorites." He glanced up at her with deep blue eyes, flecked with gold. He was younger than she'd supposed, probably not quite thirty. A light scar ran from his eyebrow to his upper lip on the right side of his face, perfectly rounded like a thin crescent moon, as though painted by a careful hand.

A burning sensation ran through Iris's own cheek, and she fought to keep from touching her face. *This man fights chains he's been bound with for years.*

"Where are my manners?" The man held out a gloved hand. "Graham Timmis."

"Ir–Isaac Fishman," said Iris, using the name she'd given at the boarding house. Her grip was firm as a man's, years of farm work had seen to that.

"I should welcome you to Emerald City, though I might have reservations if you're seeking the Burkes," Graham said. "Unless you're the bearer of some bad news for them. Nothing too terrible, mind you."

"Graham, it's scandalous the way you talk!" the old woman screeched from the carriage. "Going about and dipping your fingers in this bad blood. It's all been washed under a bridge for over a decade. Mr. Law has paid for the sins he committed, and you don't know for sure he was responsible for the worst of them. Only God knows."

"And this delightful woman," Graham rolled his eyes, "Is my Aunt Corrianne. Aunt Corrianne, meet Mr. Fishman."

"Mister?" Aunt Corrianne gave Iris a sharp look.

"Pleased to meet you," Iris said in a gruff voice. *She suspects something.*

"Tell you what, Sir," said Graham. "It's getting quite late, and bears have been seen in these parts. Why don't you sit with us in the carriage, and we can tie your horse to the back end. If you care to, you may sup with us tonight. Is that acceptable to you, Aunt Corriane?"

"If I had another preference, would you do my bidding? I think not."

Iris couldn't help but grin at the old woman's tone, she was so much like her grandma.

"I'm not sure about supper, but I will accept the ride. I'm searching for my sister. She came this way a few days ago and was to stay with the Burkes."

Graham's eyes widened. "Sister? You don't say. By the name of Fern? Fern Founder?"

Iris's heart thudded in her chest. "Yes. Have you seen her? Is she all right?"

A funny little smile lit on his lips. "She looked well to me when I met her on the road this morning. Though she had a bit of plaster bandage stuck to her forehead. I didn't ask why."

Iris let out a deep, long sigh. "Might I beg the use of an outdoor pump or well when we reach your home? I would like to make myself a bit more presentable before I reach the Burkes."

Graham grinned. "Of course you may, and a good deal better than that."

Iris tied the mare's reins to the back of the carriage. "Close to oats and a rest for you," she promised Shae.

Graham gestured inside the carriage door. "Take the empty seat, and I'll squeeze in beside you. Good thing you're a slight fellow, else we might not all fit."

Iris obeyed, sliding as close to the carriage wall as she could manage. The space was stuffy and filled with the scent of what must be Aunt Corriane's perfume. Iris was glad for it, for though she'd rinsed off before bed last night with the bucket of tepid water and lye soap provided by the establishment, the long ride through the warm spring day had done nothing for her comportment. *Good thing my hair's tucked up in my hat. It's more tangled than Granny's yarn basket.* Not that she normally cared about such things, but this was a rather fancy carriage.

"How far is the Burke ranch, and your home?" she said, trying to be gruff, yet friendly and cheerful at the same time. *Every time I open my mouth, I sound more absurd.*

"Land sakes," Aunt Corriane snapped, the feathers on her cap shaking. "You can stop the act. I know you're a woman. We've invited you to our home for dinner, so it's apparent we mean you no harm."

Graham's mouth dropped open, and he stared at his aunt with widened eyes. "What do you mean by that?" He leaned back and appraised Iris. "My good Sir, pay no heed . . ."

"I . . . I . . . she's right." Iris wanted to pull off her hat, but there wasn't room for her to do so without smacking one of her companions in the face. "I disguised myself so no one would harass me on the road. I've been riding for two days." It was Aunt Corriane's turn to be shocked. "Two days? Of all the dangerous notions. Your parents should have you horsewhipped for such an exploit. Or your husband. Haven't you heard about the bandits that have robbed several nearby towns in the last few months?"

Iris tilted her chin. "I have no husband, and no use for one–or anyone who planned to horsewhip me. The very idea! As for my mother, she trusts me to do what's best. My journey has unfolded in the utmost safety," (Except for the one incident, which Iris decided leave untold). "If I did meet a bear, I could handle it myself." She patted her deep pocket where she'd hid the tiny pistol, though Aunt Corrianne and Graham wouldn't know what she was referring to.

"All right," Graham gave a quick nod of his head. "I don't take kindly to being deceived, but under the circumstances, I understand."

"I'm sure I beg your pardon," Iris murmured, and then lapsed into a silence that engulfed the tiny carriage in a matter of moments.

She'd always been what some folks called 'an awkward child,' prone to periods of quietude. She'd only speak to strangers when spoken to, and only when pressed. The teachers of Cottage Grove's one-room schoolhouse gave up on making her recite anything. She'd stand at the front of the class, studying the other students, wondering what they pondered. She enjoyed this practice much more than trying to remember the patronizing words that filled the pages of her lesson books.

The teachers finally triumphed by giving her scriptures to

recite. These she would proclaim in confidence.

With her sisters she was different. Iris always got the four of them into scrapes, making funny faces behind the backs of visitors; only to give a serene smile while her sisters went into gales of giggles and received reprimanding looks from their mother. Though her mother's eyes always betrayed her own amusement.

The carriage hit a particularly large rock and she sat up straighter, shrugging these thoughts away. As long as her family loved and accepted her, and God poured out his love on her every day, she gave little credence to the opinions of other folks. But there was something about the way Graham studied her face, as though searching for something. *Probably trying to see the woman under all this charcoal dust.* She touched her cheek. *I wonder what he'll think of the real me?*

The coach rocked from side to side. Iris gripped the edge of her seat tighter.

"Almost there!" Graham raised his voice over the clatter. "The town has worked to fix this road for thirty years, but it hasn't helped much. Every so often, men pick up wagon loads of rocks and dump them on the side of the road, but it barely makes a dent."

"It's outrageous," Aunt Corrianne said with a sniff.

"Our roads in Cottage Grove are pretty terrible," said Iris. "Most folks wouldn't dare to own such a fancy coach. Such a vehicle would be driven to splinters in no time."

"We've reinforced the wheels and frame," said Graham. "I can assure you this coach could handle much worse."

The carriage came to a stop. "There's our gate," Graham gestured outside. "Wait here while I give the coachman a hand." The coach listed to the side as he hopped out.

Iris took a breath of fresh air before the door slammed shut. She glanced through the window, which looked out on the opposite side of the road from where the men had gone. *Perhaps I should have said no to supper. I do want to see Fern. But now I've already accepted. I don't want them to be late for their meal by having to take me to the Burke house.* She twisted a stray loop of hair around her finger. *If Fern is all right now, why did you send me here, God?* The question popped into her mind from curiosity, not from doubt. She never doubted the voice of God.

Graham hopped back in and grinned at her. "Almost home."

Only a bit of twilight at the edge of the tree line remained. Dusky purple blanketed most of the sky, studded here and there with brilliant stars. Relief whirled through Iris. *So glad I'm off the road and close to the place I need to be. But how badly is Fern hurt? And where is Carl?* She hadn't thought to ask, and Graham hadn't mentioned him.

Graham exited the coach and assisted Aunt Corrianne. He held out a hand to Iris. "Allow me, though I will get looks from my coachman, who doesn't know the joke."

Iris stared down at her fingers, encased in men's leather riding gloves several sizes too large. She pulled the gloves off and stuffed them into her pocket before taking Graham's hand.

Graham bowed as she lighted on the ground. "Welcome to our

home."

The estate before her seemed a palace, at least by size and grandeur. There was certainly nothing like it in Cottage Grove. The house sprawled out over a massive lawn, including a porch with columns too wide for a man to span with his arms. Dormer windows poked from the second story roof like the noses of inquisitive children.

"The stables are farther back behind the trees," said Graham. "My father had this place built. He raised the finest horses in Oregon, and I've carried on his legacy."

"I see," said Iris. "I do love horses."

"Glad to hear it. Please come inside and make yourself at home."

As a man in formal wear ushered them through the door, the grandeur became even more apparent. Brass candelabras flickered from ebony and mahogany furniture, and the long, wide hall ended in a stately staircase.

Aunt Corriane disappeared through a door, and the butler waved towards a coat rack. "Please, Sir, place your things there."

Oh, he's addressing me. Iris exchanged an amused glance with Graham. "Thank you. I suppose I could leave my hat here, at least."

She pulled off her battered straw monstrosity, and her hair, which she'd pinned up that morning, fell down in a soot-colored cascade around her shoulders.

The doorman's eye twitched, but to his credit, he merely

bowed and left the room.

A maid, complete with apron and frilly hat, minced towards them. "Mr. Timmis, Your aunt has informed me of our visitor."

"Yes, this is Miss Founder." Graham's eyes danced at the maid's look of surprise.

"Yes, that's right," Iris said. "If you would be so good as to show me the back door. I'm assuming you have an outside pump?"

"Nonsense." Aunt Corrianne swept back into the room. "You shall use my personal washroom. Sarah, please show her the way."

In the washroom, Iris eyed the pristine porcelain bathtub and shook her head. No time for that before dinner. But she had a wash basin and pitcher with tepid water at her disposal, and–best of all– an oval looking glass. She hastily removed her 'gunny sack clothes' as Fern always called them, washed as best she could, and slipped into one of the two clean dresses she'd packed in her carpet bag. She brushed the worst of the snarls from her knee–length hair and bound it up again in the most reasonable–looking arrangement she could manage.

She peered into the mirror. A trace of the charcoal ran along the edge of her cheek, but if she scrubbed much more, she'd remove the skin along with it.

"It's a marked improvement, anyway." She smoothed her dress, wishing she'd packed something better than her third-shabbiest calico. *Oh well, wasn't much time in the middle of the night.*

She stepped into the hallway, suddenly feeling timid. Gone

was her floppy hat to hide beneath. And no sisters walked by her side for support. *Nothing else to do.* Squaring her shoulders, she entered the dining area.

Graham stood at the head of the table, Aunt Corrianne to his right side.

When he caught sight of her, he blinked. "You–certainly look different," he stammered.

Aunt Corrianne's mouth quirked up through the wrinkles. "My dear, you are absolutely lovely." She gestured to the place setting across from her. "Sit there, so I may admire you. Goodness knows my nephew rarely entertains such lovely visitors. Mostly swarthy, smelly men here to buy his horses."

Graham gave no retort. He silently pulled out Iris's chair.

"Thank you," she said with all the decorum she could muster. She was used to having an effect on men, all her sisters were considerable beauties, but in Graham's case she found, to her surprise, that she might actually care what he thought.

She settled into her seat.

Graham bowed his head. "Dear Heavenly Father, we thank Thee . . ."

Iris's mind wandered, as it often did during long, flowery prayers. She preferred her mother and sisters' prayers, for her family believed God was right there, sitting among them, their true Father and Friend, not off in an impossible place, only listening to the fanciest of speech.

I hope Mother isn't too worried. I did leave a note.

"Miss Foster," Aunt Corriane's voice interrupted her musings. "Would you like a biscuit?"

"Oh, yes, please." Iris opened her eyes and smiled at the servant girl, who offered a basket of bread. She took one and placed it on her plate. "Forgive me if I eat quickly, but I am anxious to see my sister."

"Of course, you are," said Graham. "If I may ask, why is your sister visiting the Burke's ranch? Are you related to them somehow?"

"To the Burkes? Oh no." Iris stared at her heaping plate, wondering what to try first. "She's there on business. She left our farm with a trusted hand six days ago. Mr. Burke is interested in beekeeping. We own an extensive apiary, so she brought him some bees and stayed to show him how to care for them."

Aunt Corrianne clicked her tongue. "Not surprised at all. George Burke is always chasing after some crazy notion."

"Yes, but *bees?*" Graham contemplated a fork full of greens.

"No different than your confounded horses," Aunt Corrianne retorted.

"Horses don't sting," said Graham.

"No, but they bite and kick," said Iris.

"Mine don't," said Graham.

"We have ways of mollifying our bees as well." Iris poked at a mound of potatoes with an absurdly tiny fork she'd found among several other utensils arranged beside her plate. "If you treat them nicely, they won't sting. It's only their way of protecting themselves."

"Interesting," said Graham.

They finished the rest of the meal while Aunt Corrianne rambled on about a barn dance being held by her ladies' society in town. Graham said he'd rather muck out all his stables by himself than go, and Aunt Corrianne grumbled under her breath. It was comfortable, bickering conversation.

Iris did wonder how a handsome, wealthy man such as Graham could still be a bachelor. *People always wonder why I'm a spinster,* she reminded herself. She shuddered. Spinster was such an ugly word. Come to think of it, so was every description for a woman who'd waited too long to get married in the eyes of the world. *Old maid.* They made women like her seem like dried up old prunes, good for nothing. But as she caught a glance from Graham, she felt anything but old and wrinkled.

7
Reunion

After dinner, Iris stepped outside. A delicious coolness bathed her cheeks.

Graham followed with her carpet bag in one hand and a lantern in the other. "The Burke ranch is right down the hill. I could hitch up the carriage, but would you prefer to walk?" He gave her a sly grin. "Somehow, you seem the walking type."

Aunt Corrianne bustled to the door. "In the dark, Graham? Without a chaperone?"

Graham shrugged. "This woman has a gun in her pocket, Auntie. I'd wager that's a fairly good chaperone."

Iris raised her eyebrows. *Aunt Corrianne isn't the only one good at guessing.*

Aunt Corrianne snorted and swept back into the house, slamming the door behind her.

"Don't worry about the old girl." Graham nodded to the door.

"I'm convinced it's good for her heart to get her ire up every once in a while."

"I'll walk," Iris said. "But what about my horse?"

Graham offered his elbow. "We'll let her rest in my stables for tonight. I'll send my groom over with her tomorrow. Will that be acceptable?"

"Thank you, she does deserve a rest," said Iris.

The moon spilled light on the wide road, and wind caused the trees to sweep curtsies as Iris and Graham strolled by.

Iris's hastily pinned up hair slid from its fastenings, and she let go of Graham's elbow to fix it. He held up his lantern, making no attempt to hide his admiring stare.

Her cheeks warmed as she shoved the last pin into her mane. "Those cicadas certainly are loud tonight."

Graham tipped his head. "Yes. Haven't been this many for quite some time. Hopefully they don't affect the farmers' crops too badly."

"Does your manor have a garden?"

"A small kitchen garden," said Graham. "But mostly we grow horses. They're much more interesting than tomatoes and cabbage."

"I'm inclined to agree." Iris sidestepped to avoid a boulder the size of her head.

At the bottom of the hill was a wooden gate, painted white and wide enough for two buckboards to pass through side by side.

Graham held up the lantern, motionless.

"What's wrong?" asked Iris.

He turned back, his shoulders sagging. "I haven't gone through this gate in ten years."

"Why?"

"No matter." He slipped the lantern handle into her hands, strode forth and opened the latch. "After you, Milady."

The comforting faint scent of cattle met Iris as they walked up the driveway, and in the distance a cow lowed.

Lights twinkled from the windows of the stalwart ranch house, a much humbler building than Graham's manor. Two hounds bayed greetings, then bounded up to them, wagging their tails.

"Some guard dogs you are," said Iris, laughing. "We have a dog like that at home."

Graham rested his hand on her shoulder. "Miss Founder," he whispered, the lantern light playing on his face. "I trust you will be staying in Emerald City for a short while, at least."

"My sister planned to be here another week, to get the bees settled. And I have yet to know the extent of her injuries." Suddenly her heart bounded with a wild need to see Fern. "I really must go."

The muscles in his face slackened a bit. "Then I should be grateful for the bees. That is, if you agree to see me again. The barn social this Thursday, perhaps?"

"You made it quite clear that you hated such events."

His lip curved upward. "Ah, I did say that, didn't I? But maybe I'll find a reason to like them."

Iris's mouth was suddenly dry, and she swallowed. "Mr. Timmis, though my nature may seem forward, I can assure you I'm not given to idle dalliance."

Graham dipped his head. "Neither am I," he muttered. He took the lantern from her. "Please forgive me for staying here. A few steps to the door should see you safe. No one here will harm you, though I'd keep an eye on the younger Mr. Burke. I will take my leave."

Iris's blunt rebuttal left a sting to her lips, like chapped skin meeting salt. She'd spoken automatically, like she always did when dealing with unwanted suitors. *But he didn't deserve that. He's been nothing but kind and we had a pleasant evening. Why wouldn't I wish to visit with him again?*

But all she could say was, "Thank you for dinner."

Graham tipped his absurd hat, turned on his heel, and stalked away.

Iris watched his lantern bob down the road. *What an unusual man. And why would he have such a problem with the Burkes?*

Fern took the empty soup bowl from Carl's outstretched hand. "Looks like you had a good appetite tonight," she said in a cheery voice.

"Miss Fern, seeing you always makes my day brighter." Carl snuggled into the pile of pillows that propped him up. His leg, encased in bandages and splints up to the hip, stretched out on the mattress

A smile spread across Carl's face. "I've been feeling better, too. Doctor said my leg's mending well. No sign of sepsis."

"You're too ornery to get sepsis." Fern rested her chin on her hand. "Law sent a letter to Mother to explain what happened. But the postmaster said they keep letters saved up until they have enough to make a trip worthwhile. Sometimes it can be weeks."

Carl grunted. "Mebbie we should write her a whole sack of letters."

"Law will find another way to get word to her." Fern piled dishes on the tray and tidied books that lay scattered on the bedside table. "Don't worry too much about it. Your job is to feel better. We've only been here for four days. She won't have a reason to be worried yet."

Dogs barked outside the window. Fern peeked through the filmy muslin curtains. "Wonder what's got their dander up tonight?"

Carl shifted. "Fox in the henhouse?"

"Maybe," said Fern. "I guess I'll go make sure Law heard them. I believe he and the elder Mr. Burke are reading in the parlor."

"Them foxes are bad news." Carl gripped his pillow as though it were the neck of an offending animal. "So's a raccoon. Raccoon'll kill the whole coop full of biddies for fun."

"I'm sure everything's fine," Fern said with a sigh. She

slipped out of the room and into the empty hall.

Dim light from cracks in the closed doors was the hallway's only illumination. The ranch house had a quiet, settled air, like a mother hen resting over her nest for the night.

Mr. Burke darted past her, dressed in only long flannel underwear and a pair of battered boots. He waved an ancient musket in her direction. "Heard a commotion," he said. "Mebbie a bear after the bees."

"I wouldn't think . . ." Fern started to say, but he ran past her to the back door at the end of the hall.

"Hello, Fern. Did you hear the knock?" Law moved swiftly past her and went to the front door. He swung it open, his tall frame blocking Fern's view.

"Yes Ma'am?" Fern heard him say.

Mrs. Crenshaw emerged from the shadows and nodded towards the door. "I saw through the side window. It's a strange woman. Don't recognize her from town. Hope she's not in trouble, coming here so late at night, and alone at that." She squinted at Fern. "She has the loveliest hair . . ."

Fern pushed past Mrs. Crenshaw roughly, heedless of the shocking rudeness.

Law scooted out of the way as she barreled through the door. "Hey there." He extended his hand, but Fern paid him no heed.

"Iris," she shouted, and flung her arms around her sister. She burst into tears.

Iris squeezed her tight, then stroked her hair. "Hush now," she said. "I'm here. I was worried, but it sounds like you've been well cared for. Your poor head." She touched Fern's bandage.

"It's fine." Fern wiped tears from her cheeks. "Everything's f–fine. They've all been lovely, Law is–this is Law," she gestured to him. "What on earth are you doing here?"

Iris jutted out her chin. "I was awakened in the night. You know how it happens. God told me you were hurt, and I had to see for myself."

Law gave a low whistle. "That's uncanny."

"All of us hear from God," said Fern. "Momma calls it the Founder gift. But Iris has it the strongest."

"Well." Law rubbed his jaw. "The Bible is full of prophets and even common everyday folks who hear the voice of God. He's nudged me out of trouble more than once, I can tell you that. Come on inside, Iris Founder. Sounds like you've been on a long journey."

"Oh yes, you must be starving," Fern tugged on Iris's sleeve. "Come eat something."

"Thank you, but I've eaten," said Iris. Her gaze returned to the small bandage over Fern's eyebrow. "So you were hurt, then? Graham said he met you on the road and you seemed fine."

"Graham Timmis?" Law sputtered. "Why were you talking to Graham?

Fern's fingers crept up to the bandage. "Yes, I took a spill from the wagon. Carl suffered more than I did. His leg is broken in two places."

"Oh no!" Iris clasped her hands. "Poor Carl! Will he be all right?"

"Eventually," Fern replied. "But we can't go home until he heals, and that could be several weeks."

"Our town has the best bone-setter in Oregon," said Law. He gestured to the door. "Would you ladies please come inside now before the bears eat us alive?" He slapped his neck. "Or the mosquitoes, more likely."

"Oh, that reminds me." Fern giggled. "Your father ran out the back door to check on the bees. He thought there might be a bear."

Law shook his head. "I was joking about being eaten alive. We haven't had a bear on the farm in years." He picked up Iris's carpet bag she'd set on the porch and went inside, with Fern and Iris following.

"Please make yourself at home," said Law over his shoulder. "The spare rooms are taken but . . ."

"The bed in my room is plenty big enough for both of us, and we're used to sharing," said Fern. "Thank you so much."

They followed him down the hall to the room where Fern was staying.

"I'd take you to see Carl," said Fern as they passed his door, "But I think he's sleeping."

"I wouldn't want to disturb him." Iris brushed back a strand of hair. "I'll wait until tomorrow. After I've had a proper bath."

Law set the bag inside, then came out into the hall. "I'll just go find Father outside and explain things to him. Will you be alright?"

He glanced at Fern.

"Oh yes," she said hastily. "I'm sure my sister wants to go right to bed."

Law nodded as the two girls went into the room. "Good night." He closed the door softly.

Iris slumped into the overstuffed chair beside the bed. "I declare. What a time. Every bone in my body aches from riding the past few days." She grinned. "I haven't ridden that fast in years. Shae was dandy, though."

"I'm sure she was." Fern shook her head. "What is Mother going to think? She's probably out of her mind with worry right now."

"She knows I can handle myself." Iris twisted a loop of hair around her finger. "In my note I told her I was dressing like a man."

"You wore men's clothes?" Fern stared at her. "When did you get changed?"

"I told you, I had dinner at Graham Timmis's house." Iris sat up straight. "He's a very nice man, I don't know what problem your Law has with him."

"He's not MY Law." said Fern. Heat crept up her neck.

"Oh, isn't he?" Iris said in the infuriating, big–sister voice she rarely used anymore. She rose and swept over to the washbasin. "Do you think it would be terribly rude for me to ask for a bath this late? I tried to clean up as best I could at Graham's . . . Mr. Timmis's house."

"Oh, so now he's Graham to you, is he?" Fern meant it in a teasing way but was shocked to see a tinge of pink on her never–rattled sister.

Iris turned away, addressing a large painting of a boat on the opposite wall. "I suppose I'll have to forgo the bath tonight. I might fall asleep and drown."

Fern pulled her nightgown from the dresser drawer. *I'd better drop this for tonight, or we'll never get any rest.*

The two sisters changed, and then sat on opposite sides of the bed, brushing out their waves of hair in silence.

Fern blew out the lamp and huddled in the covers. "I still can't believe you rode all the way here by yourself. I'm glad you're safe."

"Everything was fine," Iris replied, stifling a yawn. "Mr. Timmis doesn't think much of Law. But you seem to believe he's a good person."

"He and his family have been very kind to me and Carl," replied Fern. "Law has had nothing good to say about Graham. I don't know why."

"Maybe we can find out more tomorrow," said Iris. "But first I want to see what Mr. Burke has done with our bees."

8

Sunday Conversation

Fern smoothed her Sunday best dress, a brown silk, and settled back, thankful for the blankets piled in the buckboard's bed to cushion her seat.

Emerald City's church met early. They'd finished up and were heading home before 10 o'clock.

Iris was beside her in a dress that had been borrowed from Mrs. Crenshaw, because she hadn't packed church clothes. She'd left as much space between them as possible, since the morning sun beamed bright already and the day was becoming sticky.

Fern would have insisted on walking, since the town and church were close, and she was still wary about riding in the buckboard. But Mrs. Crenshaw warned their clothes would be filthy from the dust by the time they reached the church.

The housekeeper perched on the buckboard's front seat, along with Law, who was driving. The sisters had promised to help her prepare Sunday lunch. Though Peony and Myrtle were far more accomplished cooks, Mrs. Founder had made sure all her daughters knew their way around a kitchen, preferences notwithstanding.

The church had boasted a much larger building and congregation than their own tiny place of worship in Cottage Grove. The Burkes and Timmis families each had designated pews, of course. Several looks were exchanged from both sides. A smile and a nod from Graham to Iris, glares shot between him and Law, and finally, raised eyebrows and pursed lips from Aunt Corianne and Mrs. Crenshaw. Fern felt very much as though she were in school again, and almost committed the worst offense by giggling out loud.

The worship service had been nice, the prayers dignified, and sermon meaningful, but Fern found it difficult to concentrate.

Law was so close. Alive. His bright blue shirt brought out the warmth in his skin and the sparkle in his eyes, and with every word she uttered he studied her face as though she was the most fascinating creature on earth.

She constantly wondered what he was thinking, how he felt. That he had special feelings for her was apparent, but how deep were those feelings? *And what does it matter? When Carl heals, we will go home.* This brought her back down to the worn pew with a thud. She'd shaken her head and forced herself to focus on the pastor's heartfelt, enthusiastic message.

Now in the wagon, she couldn't have remembered a word of the sermon if someone had offered her a dollar. She stole a glance at Iris. Her sister's lashes curled against her cheeks, and her lips moved in silent prayer.

Iris probably didn't remember the sermon either, but for different reasons. She was always preoccupied in her own time with God, especially when they were inside a church. Fern's relationship with God was a deep and meaningful one, but even with that, sometimes she found it difficult to understand Iris's mysterious connection with the Almighty.

The wagon jostled on the horrible stretch of road right by the house, and Fern gripped the side, wishing she'd pressed harder to walk.

As they rolled into the driveway, Mr. Burke approached the wagon, his head veiled by muslin hanging beneath his wide-brimmed hat. "Bees are lively today, Misses Founders!"

Though Fern couldn't see his face, she heard the grin in his voice.

Mrs. Crenshaw snorted. "Missed church because of your touch of gout, did you? You just wanted to spend time with your bees." She rolled her eyes. "He's going to turn heathen, girls."

Mr. Burke removed his veil and wiped his face with a large spotted handkerchief. "I happen to think spending time out of doors with God's creatures is one of the best ways to experience Him in your life."

Fern gave Iris a sideways glance. Though Iris only smiled, Fern knew her sister probably agreed with him.

Mrs. Crenshaw folded her arms. "May I remind you, Mr.

Burke, the scriptures warn us not to forsake the assembling of the brethren, and I don't think they meant bees." She turned to Law. "Perhaps you can speak some sense into your father." She pulled her hat down a bit tighter. "Come, ladies, there is much to prepare before lunch."

Fern and Iris followed her to the back of the house and the spacious kitchen. This was the first time Fern had been in this room, and she turned slowly to survey the gleaming pots and pans hanging from hooks on the wall. A large butcher's block took up the center of the room, and a massive iron stove squatted in the corner.

"I threw in a few extra logs before we left for church," said Mrs. Crenshaw. "Should be nice and warm."

"Aren't you worried about it burning the place down?" asked Iris.

Mrs. Crenshaw shrugged. "Mr. Burke and the other farmhands check on things for me." She washed her hands in a basin. "Now girls, one of you can slice bread, while the other sets out bowls. The soup has been on the back of the stove all morning."

Iris and Fern glanced at each other. "We thought you'd need more help," began Fern.

"I've fed hordes of hungry men from this kitchen by myself for the last fifteen years. I don't need assistance." Mrs. Crenshaw leaned in and gave Fern and Iris a conspiratorial wink. "I invited you two here because I know what you're dying to ask, and I'm willing to tell you about it."

Fern's mouth dropped open.

"Truly, Mrs. Crenshaw . . ." Iris began.

Mrs. Crenshaw held up a wrinkled hand. "Land sakes, child, don't you think I was your age once? I know how you girls think. You two get to work. I'll churn the butter and tell you all about why Mr. Law and Mr. Graham are mortal enemies."

She pulled the lid off the churn and poured in a pail of frothing cream. "Knives and bowls are over there." She waved to a cabinet.

"Law and Graham were thick as thieves once. Their mothers were best friends, you see, and once Law's mother passed, Mrs. Timmis stood in for her. Baked Law birthday cakes, made sure he washed behind his ears before church. I was here by then and could have taken care of those things, but I think it did him good. Both boys thought the world of her. What a woman she was! If she'd not been taken by a fever in the boys' thirteenth year, the altercations never would have gone as far as they did. She was a peacekeeper, and she would have drummed up an understanding between them."

Fern piled thick slices of bread on a platter. "How sad for them."

"Yes." Mrs. Crenshaw placed the cream pail in the washbasin. "The boys were heartbroken, as you could imagine. They attended school together, and as they grew, their attentions turned to what most men's eventually do."

She slapped the lid on the churn and pumped the dasher up and down. "A girl came along."

"Here, I'm finished with the bowls. Let me do that," said Iris, taking the dasher handle.

"Thank you, dearie." Mrs. Crenshaw wiped her face and sat on a stool. "Now where was I? Oh. The girl. Elmira Greer. She was a pretty little thing, though not as fair as the two of you. She stole both those boys' hearts right out of their chests and locked them in a jar, like butterflies. One look at their faces and anyone would have seen they were both madly in love.

"Without mothers, the boys both confided in me. Graham honored their friendship and kept his feelings in his heart, refusing to try for the girl. But Law couldn't stand the prick of Cupid's bow. He asked Elmira to sit with him at the school picnic." She chuckled. "Might as well have asked for her hand in marriage, at least in grade school."

"Graham must have been upset," said Fern.

"Oh, more than upset. Though the boys didn't mention a word of the situation to each other, Graham swore he'd never forgive Law for his betrayal. And even though Elmira Greer moved away with her family to California a year later, he hasn't spoken a word to Law since."

"Surely he's forgiven him by now," said Fern. *How petty Graham must be.*

Iris paused with the churn, staring down at the floor.

"I'm almost certain he would have." Mrs. Crenshaw tapped her chin. "If something worse hadn't happened a few months after Elmira moved away. The boys were sixteen. A man bought a prized stallion from the Timmis ranch. Paid a fortune. But the beast picked up a stone shortly after and became lame. The man didn't care for his horses like the Timmis stables. The lameness went untreated, and horse was put down."

"How sad," said Iris, who had given up churning altogether.

Fern gazed at the motionless knife in her hands and back to Mrs. Crenshaw.

"Anyway, the man blamed Graham's daddy for selling him a lame horse. Mr. Timmis refused to give him back his money."

Mrs. Crenshaw pursed her lips. "Law was at home sick with a cold while Mr. Burke and I were in town running errands. The other farm hands were out in the fields. Law smelled smoke from the house. When he stepped outside, an eerie orange glow came from over the hill. As he ran up the road to the Timmis farm, he realized the stables were on fire."

"Oh dear," Fern breathed.

"The rains had been absent for some weeks, and Law knew a pailful of water at a time from the well wouldn't do much. He heard the screams of the frightened horses, so he pulled off his shirt and brought them out, one at a time, by covering their heads with the cloth."

"He managed to save three before seeing another figure struggling in the smoke. Graham.

"Law screamed a warning, but part of a stall collapsed and hit Graham's head, knocking him out cold."

Iris clasped her hands. "What did Law do?"

Mrs. Crenshaw signed. "The only thing he could do. Pulled Graham out and tried to revive him. By then the barn had collapsed and the other two steeds perished. The only fortunate thing was that most of the horses were out in the fields."

"Law saved Graham's life." Fern grip on the knife tightened. "Why would he still be so angry?"

Mrs. Crenshaw shook her head. "Anger does strange things to people. Graham escaped with a few bruised ribs and a burn on his face. You might have seen the scar?" She glanced at Iris.

Iris nodded. "The one that looks like a crescent moon?"

"Yes. No one knows how the fire was started, but the sheriff believed it was caused by a man. Because Law was there, Graham thinks he's responsible."

"That's ridiculous." Fern snorted. "Why would Law have stayed and tried to save the horses?"

Mrs. Crenshaw shrugged. "Who knows what put that notion into Graham's head? Like I said, anger does strange things to people."

Fern glanced at Iris, who had gone back to churning. Her sister's face was red, and the muscles in her cheeks twitched. Rarely did she see Iris show so much emotion. *Could she have feelings for Graham?* Her shoulders sagged. *After all the men who've fallen for her, she had to pick the one who hates Law.*

Why would I care about that? But the more she thought about it, the more she did.

###

After lunch the menfolk settled by the fire, reading periodicals or whittling.

Fern spent half an hour reading to Carl, and then she led Iris out to see the bees. Sunshine filtered through the leaves and gleamed on spiderwebs in the weeping willow trees beside the hives.

"He chose a pleasant location." Iris circled the five hives with their still-fresh wood. "These appear to be tight and dry."

"Mr. Burke has done his research." Fern adjusted her muslin veil. "They seem to be settling in nicely. The only challenge has been to keep Mr. Burke away and let them alone. They need a few days to themselves."

"Remember when we first built our hives?" Iris said. "Mother couldn't keep us away either."

"I remember." Fern removed two curled leaves that had fallen in front of a hive's entrance. "These ladies have a good home here. Mr. Burke isn't out to make a fortune. He simply wants to have them around. He refers to them as his little friends."

Iris studied the hive's opening, where buzzing bees clustered together. "That's exactly what they are, but few people think of them in that way." She tilted her head. "What about Law?"

"What about him? He's not really into bees, if that's what you mean."

"That's not what I mean." That light was in Iris's eyes.

She knows something. Something she's not telling me. Fern sucked in a breath. This often happened when Iris heard the voice of the Lord. She'd 'let the words steep,' as she called it, keeping it in her heart until she felt free to share the message.

Curiosity surged through Fern's veins, but she knew better than to ask. Iris would tell her when the time was right.

Iris's gaze was unflinching, so Fern finally shrugged. "I don't know, Iris. He's a sweet man. And considerate. He quotes poetry."

"There you go," said Iris. "He's your perfect match." The words were teasing, but her jaw was set.

Fern stepped away from the hives. "We'd better let the ladies continue to work. They have their combs to finish."

"Indeed." Iris put a hand on her hip. "Hard to believe Graham thinks that Law would start that barn fire."

"He'd just lost his mother," Fern reminded her. "And he was very young."

"Yes."

As they walked back to the house, Law came out to meet them. He still wore his Sunday best shirt, but his sleeves were rolled up to the elbows.

"Hello." He gave Fern a smile. "With the flurry that always comes on Sundays, I forgot to tell you ladies . . . since you're going to be here a while, you're invited to the dance Thursday night. There'll be a barn raising first. The ladies come and cook, and the men work together to construct the building. After that, everyone goes home to clean up and then we gather at a neighboring barn for a dance. In Mrs. Crenshaw's words, it should be a 'hoot.'"

That look came into his eyes, and he quoted,

"Oh, what delight when the youthful and gay
Each with eye like a sunbeam and foot like a feather,
Thus dance, like the Hours to the music of May,
And mingle sweet song and sunshine together."

"Except it will be nighttime, but the sentiment still stands," he added.

Iris turned away, and Fern knew she was probably stifling a laugh. Law's use of poetry was over the top, but she found herself looking forward to his random quotes.

She tapped Iris's shoulder. "What do you think? We could at least help cook during the day."

"Of course we'll help cook," Iris said. She picked at her pleated skirt. "But I already had to borrow this dress from Mrs. Crenshaw, and the style's not really suitable for a woman my age. Not to mention I'm swallowed up in all this fabric, since she's several sizes larger. My other ones are dreadfully shabby and yours aren't nice enough for an evening dance either. What on earth will we wear?"

"You want to go to the dance?" Fern gasped.

Law rubbed his chin. "To me, you ladies look lovely in what you're wearing now, but I'd want you to feel comfortable. Mrs.

Crenshaw might help. Her daughter lives nearby and is quite fashionable–at least that's what Mrs. Crenshaw says. I know nothing of such things. She might have dresses you two can borrow."

Fern opened her mouth to object, but Iris spoke first. "I'm sure we can figure out something. We would love to accompany you. Gives us something to look forward to."

What has gotten into Iris? Fern stared after her sister as she continued to the house. Iris would usually rather clear the rocks from a freshly plowed acre than go to such a function. Though she certainly was the most graceful dancer of the four sisters.

Iris lifted her skirts and swept away over the yard. Fern decided not to press the issue. One never knew with Iris.

9
Raising Trouble

Iris placed the bushel basket of biscuits down and gave the flour sack cover a little pat. The two sisters and Mrs. Crenshaw had spent all morning kneading, rolling, cutting them out, and baking. She'd lost count of how many they'd made.

If only we had a jar of honey. But the bees hadn't been settled long enough to produce more than a few teaspoons' worth.

She picked at the lace on the collar of her borrowed dress. Though the sprigged lavender was lovely, she detested lace. Hopefully, the gown Mrs. Crenshaw had borrowed for the dance wouldn't be so itchy. *Should be more grateful.*

Other calico-clad women from the town bustled to the row of tables, set up in the shade of several cottonwood trees. They brought platters and baskets and pans heaped with boiled potatoes, fried chicken, cakes and beans, each dish giving off a more mouth-watering aroma than the last.

Fern nudged her. "Have you ever seen so many pies?" she whispered.

"More than the Christmas church social back home," Iris whispered back. "The lemon chiffon pie brought by the pastor's wife seems especially toothsome."

"I hate that word." Fern wrinkled her nose. "Always makes me think of when I had that toothache and Mother made me keep that giant poultice in my cheek."

"You looked like a prairie dog." Iris giggled.

Mrs. Crenshaw approached them. "If you're finished there, ladies, I would like to introduce you to some of my friends." She lowered her voice. "They're from the Methodist church. But they're delightful souls, nonetheless."

Iris rolled her eyes. She'd never understood the stigma that some people placed on different denominations. *We all love Jesus. Isn't that what's important?*

But she dutifully followed Mrs. Crenshaw's bobbing hat through the crowd.

Mrs. Crenshaw approached three middle-aged women, all plump with plume-bestowed hats. "Girls, this is Mrs. Lavinia, Mrs. Collins and Miss Portant."

Mrs. Levinia held a monocle up to one eye. "Ah, the bee ladies from the north. How do you do?"

Iris took the offered gloved hand of Miss Portant. "Fine, thank you."

Mrs. Collins shuddered beneath her thin shawl. "Imagine

caring for little winged bugs that sting! Ladies, I don't know how you do it."

Iris attempted to find a reply, but she was interrupted by Miss Portant's gasp. "Ladies, I do declare! Is that Graham Timmis? He never comes to these sorts of events."

Iris reminded herself to turn her head in a slow, nonchalant manner, though her heart pounded.

There he is. Work clothes had replaced his formal garb, and he and his groom worked together with a two-man saw, cutting long planks into smaller pieces. A few yards away, Law and his farmhand, Richard, were doing the same task.

The men had gathered on the other side of the yard where trees had been felled and the ground prepared for new stables. Years ago, they would have built the walls from hand-hewn boards, but in this case a stack of gleaming lumber from a factory awaited construction. Over three dozen fellows busied themselves measuring, sawing and setting out strings to make sure the walls were straight.

Fern's gaze was fixed on Law, and a tiny smile played on her lips.

Mrs. Levinia leaned closer to Fern. "And you, dearie, going through that terrible accident? I live next door to the doctor. His wife told me it was the Lord's miracle you aren't up to join the angels by now!"

Fern's fingers crept up to the bandage on her forehead. "Y– yes, I'm thankful to be alright."

"You must have been so scared when that horse ran away with you!" Miss Portent pressed her palm against the ample broach pinned to her dress. "I don't know how you'll ever get in a wagon again."

Fern smiled a bit too brightly. "I'm sure I don't know, but I had to travel to church somehow, didn't I? Mrs. Crenshaw, do you think it's time to make that lemonade?"

Mrs. Crenshaw's lips twisted up in the corners. "I suppose. Those men'll be swaggering over here for something cold to drink soon enough. T'was lucky your trees are still producing," she said to Mrs. Levinia."

"Certainly," said Mrs. Levinia. "We had so many we provided them for the wedding a week ago. Pity you couldn't come, Mrs. Crenshaw. Ginny Dawson was a lovely bride."

"That was the day this sweet girl crashed in front of our farm," said Mrs. Crenshaw, patting Fern on the hand. "I was fine missing it, considering."

"You never know." Miss Portant gave a mysterious smile. "There might be another wedding before we know it."

Fern smiled back, and Iris blinked. *She doesn't realize they're talking about her. These ladies don't miss a thing.*

Sweat trickled down Iris's back. "Ladies, please excuse me. My head is aching ever so slightly. I believe a few moments in the shade would do me good."

She glided over to a spot under the trees and fanned herself with a broad maple leaf. Taking in deep breaths, she closed her eyes. She never was one for crowds, and the heat didn't help much.

A group of younger girls nearby cared for the littlest children; some barely toddling around. They worked together to make play houses with scraps of wood.

A man strode up to her shelter in the trees. Though he looked past thirty, his limbs were long and gangly, like a teenager that hadn't quite grown into himself. His blond hair was slicked back and scruffy, hanging over his ears like old hay. A trimmed goatee sprouted from his chin, and he wore a rather stringy tie that seemed to be the fashion in this town.

He removed his round straw hat. "I don't believe I've had the pleasure of making your acquaintance." He talked through his teeth, causing a strange whistling sound with each word.

"Iris Founder," she said shortly, while he took her hand and bowed.

"Harry Wiley," he replied. "I'm the mayor of Emerald City."

"Pleased to meet you." *Forgive me for lying, God, I could have gone my entire life happily without meeting this man.* She pulled back her hand and craned her neck in a pointed fashion, trying to glimpse the industrious woodworkers.

He licked his lips and pushed his hands into his pockets, rocking on his heels. "I'm here to oversee the building, since it's within the town limits and all. We focus on proper construction. Don't want the entire structure crashing down to brain someone."

Iris squinted at the stable's framework, which was coming together rapidly, in her estimation. "It looks solid enough to me."

"Are you coming to the dance tonight?" Mayor Wiley blurted.

"I plan to, yes," said Iris. "Now, if you'll excuse me, I must see if the ladies need my help."

As she turned away, he let out a huffing noise she recognized well as the indignation of a suitor not accustomed to rebuttal.

Mrs. Crenshaw plucked at Iris's sleeve as she returned to the drink table, where Fern was squeezing lemons. "Why were you talking to the mayor?" she hissed.

"Couldn't help it," Iris said. "He spoke to me first."

"More's the pity." Mrs. Crenshaw put a hand on a hip. "He's the one suspected of helping his father burn down the Timmis barn all those years ago. No one could prove anything, mind you."

"Then how did he become mayor?" asked Fern, who was now listening to the conversation with clasped hands and shining eyes.

Mrs. Crenshaw shook her head. "Money and bad behavior will buy you more than you could imagine."

Whooping and hollering sprang up from the stable site, and the women ran to check on the commotion like a flock of colorful geese.

Iris found herself in the front, with Fern at her elbow.

Graham and Law continued to saw wood with their partners, but another pair of workers had joined in the task. Mayor Wiley controlled one end of a saw, and a squat, burly fellow she didn't recognize gripped the other. They appeared to be in a contest, for all six men sawed like their lives depended on it. Three groups of enthusiastic boys fed them boards, which were quickly sawed and added to three piles of completed pieces.

A small boy skipped by and hollered, "Twenty to eighteen to sixteen with Mr. Timmis ahead. First one to thirty wins!"

"Go Law!" Mr. Burke shouted from the sidelines. The crowd took up the chant, with different folks yelling the name of their desired champion.

Iris watched in breathless excitement. Surely Graham would win. Sweat poured down his face from beneath the brim of his silly hat, and his mouth was set in a determined line. His broad shoulders rose and fell with each movement of the saw.

Law whistled a merry tune as he worked, shoving the freshly sawed boards to the side with his boot as they fell.

Mayor Wiley glanced at Iris, who turned her head with a sniff. *Is he really trying to impress me? The very idea!*

When she glanced his way once more, he was hunched over his saw, scarlet creeping into his gaunt cheeks.

The crowd counted along now, as each board fell. Twenty-five to twenty-three to twenty-seven in Graham's favor.

Down to the last board. Fern gripped Iris's arm so tight she felt sure she'd have a bruise. The men set their blades to the wood; the blades biting into the grain.

The whine of metal filled the air. A thin piece of steel whipped out, slicing into Graham's arm. He jumped away from the saw with a yelp as blood spattered his crisp white shirt sleeve. His groom also moved quickly but appeared unhurt.

Iris's heart leapt to her throat, and she stood on her tiptoes to get a better look.

Law's board hit the ground with a satisfying crunch, and cheers erupted from the crowd. Fern squealed and clapped her hands, then gave Iris's arm a pat. "Hope Graham's all right."

Mayor Wiley threw his saw on the ground and stalked off behind the stables.

Iris pressed forward, trying to reach Graham through the crowd, but Law got to him first.

"Is it deep?" He reached for the bleeding arm. "The doctor isn't far; I saw him cross the yard a few minutes ago."

"I'm fine." Graham jerked his arm away and turned to leave. He locked eyes with Iris.

She found herself tumbling into the blue depths, doubts and wonder swirling through her thoughts. *Will you allow God to break your chains of unforgiveness and heal you? What do you truly think of me?*

He gave a curt nod, breaking the spell. "Miss Founder." His boots crunched on the rocky ground as he stalked away, clutching his wrist.

Law's eyes narrowed. "Wasn't more than a scratch," he said to Iris and Fern as he removed his hat and wiped away sweat.

"He didn't have to be so unpleasant," said Fern.

Law shrugged. "I'm used to it," he said. A sadness crept into his eyes. "I'd better get back to work, ladies, these stables won't build themselves."

The men returned to their tasks, and the women finished

organizing the lunch. Graham didn't return for the meal. Despite his sullen attitude, Iris carried the satisfaction of how hard he'd worked. He'd proved to be more than a pampered dandy.

As they cleaned up after lunch, she whispered to Fern, "We would have won that competition, hands down, if only we'd had a saw."

10
Night Dance

Iris hesitated beneath the massive barn door, which was wide enough for a buckboard to trundle in and out with ease. Light from dozens of lanterns flickered on the rough-hewn walls. Garlands woven from asters, daisies and fleabane were draped over every peg and shelf, hiding the more mundane farm implements. They perfumed the air, masking otherwise unsavory odors one would usually find in a barn.

Farmers, shopkeepers and businessmen stood in groups talking about crops, money, and daily life. Older women relaxed on logs and hay bales along the walls, while younger women stood to the sides, eyeing eligible bachelors behind their fans. Herds of children darted through the chaos, headed to whatever adventures that awaited outside in the twilight.

A band, comprised of a fiddler, harmonica player, and an old fellow who blew on a jug, played a rollicking rendition of "Turkey in the Straw" on the far side of the barn, and several couples were already dancing.

Iris took a deep breath. Sometimes crowds made her anxious. She preferred to attend small gatherings. The outdoor potluck from this morning had been different; it was outside with plenty of open places for her to migrate to when needed.

Graham might come. Thoughts of him had filled her mind throughout the afternoon as she and Fern had prepared for the dance. The day's activities had failed to push him away, even when she spent time with her beloved bees.

The borrowed dress was splendid. Mrs. Crenshaw's daughter, who lived in town, had married a rich sea merchant and possessed excellent taste. The merchant supplied his wife with the latest European fashions, some of which Fern and Iris politely declined for decorum's sake, as the necklines plunged most scandalously. The chosen dresses were lovelier than anything the girls owned, though Peony was a brilliant seamstress. They simply hadn't the occasion to wear anything so fine until that night.

Iris's dress was purple taffeta, with blue and black accents in the ruffles and wide sleeves that Mrs. Crenshaw called 'leg o' lamb.' The stiff fabric made her arms itch, but she had to admit it set off her grey eyes and light skin perfectly. The green and gold poplin Fern wore brought out the golden highlights in her hair, which had been piled into soft curls with a rope of pearls twisted around them.

"Are you ever going in?" whispered Fern from behind her

Iris stepped through the barn's entrance with tentative steps. The tantalizing aroma of baked goods (where the women had found time to cook more food she couldn't guess) filled the air, and suddenly, she was glad she'd come.

The change in atmosphere from earlier in the day was tangible. Laughter filled the air, and smiles were friendly and warm. Everyone had changed from work clothes to polished, stiff, bright, more-than-Sunday best.

As Iris inched past the crowd, several young men attempted to catch her eye, and a few of the bolder fellows edged closer, giving Law, who stood at her elbow, glowering looks. *Law isn't who you should worry about, at least where I'm concerned.* Fern, on the other hand . . . one look at her face when she talked with Law and any simpleton could tell she was *far gone* as they used to say when they were little girls.

Her eyes flitted over the crowd. Graham was nowhere to be seen. Her shoulders slumped, and she silently chastised herself. *Silly Iris, he's a rich gentleman. What would he want with a poor farm girl like you?* This blistering thought led to irritation. Her mother and sisters lived comfortably compared to many folks, thanks to their flourishing crops and bees. And she'd turned down offers from much wealthier men in her day. She'd always longed for a man who lived by the adage that 'beauty is vain, but a woman who fears the Lord should be praised.' And so far, though men had gushed over her beauty and compared her eyes to every celestial body imaginable, including the light of Venus, not one of them had ever asked about her relationship with God. And He was, besides bees, and maybe horses, the only thing she really cared to discuss. Her faith was the glowing center of her life, a shining beacon that kept her from floating away to the darkest places of her mind. *Does Graham care about God?* He seemed so wrapped up in the old grudge.

"Would you care to dance?" A voice, with a hint of a strange whistle, disturbed her thoughts.

Her heart skipped a beat, but quickly plummeted as she swiveled her head. It wasn't Graham Timmis at all, but Mayor Wiley.

"I was hoping you'd come this evening," he said, touching her ungloved hand, his thin moustache twitching like a praying mantis catching prey. "I intended to request you save me a dance earlier today, but you darted off so quickly I didn't have a chance."

Iris hadn't considered dancing with anyone, except perhaps Law or Graham, should they ask. Her stomach twisted at the thought of being in such close proximity to the mayor. She checked over her shoulder for Law and Fern, but they were nowhere to be seen.

"I arrived moments ago." She dipped her head. "Allow me to get my bearings."

His face reddened a tinge, but he gave a curt nod. "As you wish." He moved away.

Iris wiped her palm with a handkerchief, trying to rid her skin of the slimy sensation the man had left behind. *Bearings or not, he won't be getting a dance from me this evening.*

Fern swooped by on Law's arm, eyes sparkling. They skipped off towards the dancers.

Now you show up. She twisted her hands, wondering how soon was too soon to go off in search of pie.

"Good evening." Graham's voice broke through the friendly chatter and fiddle music.

Iris's heart jumped right up in her throat and stuck there, fluttering like a moth. She spun around.

He still sported a flat-brimmed hat, though this one shone brighter than the one he'd worn earlier today. A slight bulge on his arm beneath his jacket reminded her of his injury. Like Law had suggested, the wound must not have been serious.

"H-hello. I didn't know if you were coming," she stammered, hating how flustered she sounded.

"I almost didn't." He adjusted the wrists of his cream-white gloves. "But I didn't get a chance to speak to you earlier today. I thought…" a rare grin swept over his face. "I thought it might be wonderful to see you dance."

His tone was light, the glowering mood from earlier in the day gone. He gave a bow, formal, but filled with warmth, so different from that of Mayor Wiley, who now glared at her from the corner.

"Would you care to dance?" Graham asked.

For the first time since third grade, when she'd fallen hopelessly in love with little David Shafto, she felt an irresistible draw to a man. His face was stoic, composed, but his pleading eyes betrayed his hope.

"Of course," she murmured.

He led her through the crowd. A few folks stared, and one fellow's jaw dropped. *Probably wondering about the strange girl on the arm of one of the wealthiest men in town.* But she didn't care.

They floated to the dance floor, where the crowd partook of a lively quadrille. Iris had learned several of the steps with her sisters, and the caller gave plenty of time for the crowd to adjust to each new movement.

This was far more to Fern's liking than hers, and true to form, Fern and Law galloped through two rows of clapping town folks. Fern's cheeks were red, and her hair, so carefully pinned before, had tumbled around her shoulders.

Law danced without hesitation, obviously skilled in this art.

Iris tipped her head, waiting for Graham to lead her into the mayhem.

He stared at the dancers. "I believe there's a waltz next. Would you care to wait for that one?"

"Fine with me." Iris gave a sigh of relief. *Either he is like me, or he senses my feelings about crowds. Whichever it is; it's nice.*

"The night is beautiful. Why don't we walk this way until the music changes?" He led her through the back door that faced the new stable, which, despite interruptions for a certain wood cutting competition, had been mostly completed. The fresh scent of new lumber filled the air.

The buggies were parked in the road, so they were spared the odors of horses and manure, and flies were minimal. Only a few errant children, on their way to mischief, disturbed the silence.

"The moon is lovely," said Iris, and indeed it was. Full and round, golden like a jar filled with honey. Fireflies glowed love messages amongst the buildings.

"I meant what I said." Graham didn't let go of her hand. "Rather presumptuous of me, I suppose, but I wanted to see you again." His voice dropped, almost to a whisper. "Needed to see you again."

She struggled for composure as all sorts of outrageous thoughts flooded her mind. Kings in her mother's fairy tales that married the first eligible maiden simply to produce an heir or break a curse. The ridiculous men who'd "come a'courtin' for 'any one a t'four" because they believe Mrs. Founder would jump at the chance for a man to head the farm. *Could Graham possibly be sincere?* Usually, her gift of discernment served her well in times like these, but now she felt no sense of danger, no unease. Of course, passions of the human heart could cloud her judgement, and right now hers felt like it was being squeezed. The feelings contained within burst forth and flowed through her soul.

"I'm sorry." Graham released her hand and rubbed his jaw. "I know this is hardly decorum. I know so little about you. I've never acted in such a presumptuous manner."

"That's all right," she said, her words so automatic she briefly wondered if she'd been the one to utter them.

"But I want to find out, do you understand?" Graham gazed into her eyes. "I want to know absolutely everything about you. The first words you uttered as a child. Do you like cats? What are your feelings about milk and molasses?"

She stared up at the moon. "Quite a range of subjects. I'm not sure where to start."

He cupped a hand behind his ear. "The music's still lively. Shall we wait a while longer?"

"Yes, please. I'm not one for crowds."

"Neither am I," he said. He reached down and gathered up a handful of pebbles, then tossed them one at a time, watching them bounce along the dirt. "Well. What does Iris Founder love?"

"I like bees. I am very close to my sisters, and to God . . ." she took a deep breath. *Might as well tell the truth.* "I like climbing trees."

"Climbing trees?" He gave a short laugh, glanced at her face, and sobered. "I'm sorry. I didn't mean to be rude; your answer was so unexpected! I suppose I shouldn't be surprised. Any woman who dresses like a man and comes galloping in to rescue her sister would naturally have an aboral inclination. Besides trees, what do you like? Riding bears in the races, I suppose."

"Now you're just teasing." She put a hand on her hip. "I'm half tempted not to speak to you again." She turned her nose up, her cheeks flaming as she did so. *And now I'm flirting! What on Earth would Myrtle and Peony say? They'd say I'd lost my mind, that's what.*

Graham dropped the rest of the pebbles. "Oh, you won't get rid of me that easily." His tone was teasing, but the intensity was back in his stare.

The notes of a waltz floated through the barn doors and into the night sky, wrapping themselves around the moon.

"Are you ready?" asked Graham, offering his arm.

"'I suppose." She tucked her hand around the fine velvet sleeve of his waistcoat.

He led her to just inside the door, slightly apart from the thickest crowd, and took her hand in his. Mother had taught all the girls to waltz, but it had been a while, and Iris stumbled through the first steps.

"Sorry." She laughed. "I used to be better."

"No matter." Graham pulled her closer. "If you can trust me, I'll show you the way."

Iris followed his swift, graceful movements, and in moments she'd remembered the old patterns. Her head was level with his shoulder, and she breathed in the spicy scent of cedars, with a dash of horse.

A loud voice at her shoulder broke her reverie.

"Good evening, Mr. Timmis," Mayor Wiley said, in a tone sharp enough to cut a boulder. "Wouldn't expect you to mingle with the commoners."

Graham stepped back, his eyebrows drawing together over his nose. "If I'd known you were coming, I might've changed my mind."

The mayor smirked. "Wish you would have, then I'd have this stunning creature all to myself." He gave Iris a raking stare. "She owes me a dance."

Iris opened her mouth, but Graham cut in before she could speak. "I doubt she wants to be called a creature."

Mayor Wiley grabbed her elbow. "We'll just see. It's my turn to dance, at any rate."

Graham's grip on her hand tightened. "She doesn't want to dance with you," he said through gritted teeth.

"I also don't take kindly to being spoken about as though I wasn't here." Iris glared at both the men. "I'll thank you to unhand me."

She jerked her arms free and stalked away from both men.

Graham touched her arm, and she swung to face him, cheeks flaming.

"I'm-I'm terribly sorry," he stammered. "Mayor Wiley and I have . . . well, there's bad blood, and my ire gets up when I see him."

"Seems that's a problem you have with many people," said Iris, coolly.

His eyes fell. "No, you've seen the worst, truly. I'm sorry for allowing you to be in the middle of that. I–could we finish our waltz?"

Blood pounded in her head, and a sudden dizziness made her miss a step. Her arm burned where Mayor Wiley had pinched the skin.

"You'll have to forgive me. I'm not in a mood for dancing," she replied, and staggered through the crowd to find Fern.

"Wait, Iris, please . . ." His voice was soon drowned by dozens of other conversations.

Her sister sipped punch amid a group of women, one of whom was Mrs. Crenshaw.

Fern glanced her way and almost dropped her cup. "Iris! Whatever is the matter?"

Iris clenched her hands to stop them from shaking. Her skin burned. *I must look a sight. What is wrong with me?*

"I'm not feeling well. I believe it would be best for me to go home."

"Goodness!" Mrs. Crenshaw's eyebrows travelled up to the brim of her straw bonnet. "I hope it's nothing serious."

Fern took Iris's arm. "I'm sure you're fatigued from the day; we were in the heat for most of the time. I'll walk with you to the carriage. Mrs. Crenshaw, do you think we could drive it home alone? I'd hate to keep Law from the rest of the dance."

"Nonsense." Law appeared at Fern's elbow, concern in his eyes. "We'll leave for home together at once."

"Oh." Iris pressed her hand against her cheek. "I'm so sorry to spoil your evening. Perhaps I should sit for a bit and drink some punch."

Law shook his head. "Absolutely not. I have to brand calves first thing in the morning, so I never planned to make this a late night. He gave Fern a swooning glance. "I'll bring the buggy around."

"Thank you so much, Law," said Fern, who actually batted her eyelashes.

"Yes, thank you," said Iris, though she already regretted her hasty reaction. *I could be waltzing this very moment.* But the dizzy, sick feeling wouldn't go away, and she couldn't shake her irritation. If there was one thing she couldn't stand, it was men speaking over her head as though she wasn't even a person.

Safely home, and with splendor traded for nightgowns, the sisters lounged on the floor beside the fireplace in their room.

"Can you tell me why you really wanted to come home tonight?" Fern asked. "I don't think I've ever seen you so angry, not even when Billy Phillips tormented that kitten of yours."

Iris shuddered. "Billy was the most odious boy ever created. Mayor Wiley is a close second." She told Fern what happened.

"No wonder you're so upset." Fern gave her a hug. "I would have acted in the same fashion; except I probably would have burst into tears and spoiled my dress."

Iris stroked the voluminous skirt of the gown she'd worn, which hung nearby. "At least I didn't do that. I wanted to slap them both. Why do things have to be this way? Why can't humans be like the creatures that mate for life, knowing instantly when they find the right person?"

"I don't know." Fern plucked a stray feather from the pillow in her lap. "Maybe you're just used to knowing things ahead of time. For some reason God wants to reveal His purpose in little bits, like He does for most of us. Maybe He wants to bring some excitement to your life."

"Ha." said Iris. "I mean, maybe. But I'm all rumpled and unsettled, and I don't care to feel that way."

"So am I." Fern smiled and glanced away, her cheeks tinged with pink.

"I wasn't sure at first, but Law seems like a good man," said Iris. "I really believe it's impossible he could have set fire to that barn. He was kind to bring us home tonight like he did."

Fern clasped her hands. "Oh, do you think so? I was hoping you would agree! Your opinion means more to me than . . . even Mother's!"

Joy bubbled within Iris, despite the disaster of the evening. "I truly do think he's your match in every way. But Fern?"

"Yes, Iris?"

"What will I ever do without you?"

Fern's mouth quirked downward. "Though Law has expressed fondness for me, he hasn't been clear about his intentions."

Iris wrapped her arms around Fern's shoulders. "He's in love with you. A mole in a darkened cellar could see that."

Fern flushed. "Maybe so."

"I'm sure he'll share those intentions before we head home."

"What would I say?" Fern rose and paced across the room.

"How could I leave the farm and all of you?"

"Mother never intended for us to stay forever." The realization dawned on Iris, even as she spoke. "She's prepared us for the outside world, to stand strong on our own two feet. She just wanted us to be choosy about who we spent our lives with, so we could avoid as much misery as possible."

"Mother certainly wasn't choosy." Fern sat on the bed and rested her chin on her hands. "She married the first man who proposed to her."

"Yes, and by a miracle, they were happy," said Iris. "But that doesn't mean we should follow her example. Times were very hard for them."

"I suppose we'll see how everything plays out," said Fern.

Iris tried to swallow the lump in her throat. Every prophetic bone in her body told her what would happen. And she was happy for her sister. *But how will I leave her behind?*

11
A Walk in the Woods

Bees flicked in and out of the small entrance to the wooden hive, built so carefully by Mr. Burke's patient hands. Fern raised the smoker higher while Iris slid out a drawer near the top.

"Any signs of growth?" Fern peered over Iris's shoulder.

"Plenty." Iris held up the comb, the swarming black and orange clusters of bees still working frantically despite the invasion. She pointed to several small hexagons, almost too small to see. "There, Mr. Burke. These are the kinds of things we want to see. New eggs and new larvae."

Mr. Burke clapped and leaned forward. "Oh, I am pleased! And happy that you stayed longer. I've learned so much from you both."

"I'm sure Carl would quibble about staying longer," Iris said dryly.

Mr. Burke's moustache quivered. "Oh, that's not what I

meant, of course. I'm very thankful Mr. Carl is on the mend."

"Of course that's what you meant." Fern patted his hand and frowned at Iris.

Law approached the group under the trees, his hands in his pockets.

"Good morning." Fern's heart gave a little jolt. She hadn't seen Law so far today. When the sisters had come to the breakfast table, Mrs. Crenshaw said Law had slipped out to the pasture before dawn to help with a calving.

His hands and clothes were clean now, so he must have gone back to the house to change before coming here. No wonder. Even the easiest calving was a messy business.

"Did Flossie do well?" Mr. Burke asked, his eyes never leaving his bees.

"As you suspected." Law grinned. "Two bouncing baby boys. Was a task to bring them here, but they both look strong and are eating heartily."

Mr. Burke nodded. "Flossie calved twins a few years back, and she never had trouble keeping up with them. Only t'was girls, that time."

Law sidled up to Fern. "Want to join me for a morning walk before we bore you to death with ranch talk?"

"It doesn't bother me, remember?" Fern replaced the lid of the hive she'd been inspecting.

"I'll have to show you the new claves sometime soon," said Law. "They're rambunctious little things already."

"They sound delightful." Fern removed her muslin veil. "Let me finish settling this last hive."

"I'll do it," said Iris. "Why don't you go? I'd like a bit of time to myself this morning." A mischievous glint came into her eye. "There's a giant spruce in the north pasture I'd like to climb."

Law laughed. "A favorite of mine. Though I haven't scaled it since I was oh, twelve, maybe?" He nodded to Fern. "What do you say?"

"Let me drop off these bee clothes at the house." Fern moved away from the hive and removed her gloves.

Thick grass swished around her ankles, tugging on the hem of her dress. The scents of hay and sunshine filled the air, and grasshoppers flew before her through the grass, wings clicking.

She glanced back at Iris, still discussing bees with Mr. Burke. Law tilted his head, for once appearing to be interested in the conversation.

All things considered; she was thankful Iris had come. Yes, her mother had generously chosen Fern to take the journey and Fern knew plenty about hives and honey, but Iris was the true bee expert.

After reaching the shed beside the house where they kept bee equipment, she stacked her gloves and hat on a shelf and attempted to pat her hair into place.

When she emerged, Law was leaning against the side of the house. His dark gray shirt matched his hat, and his beard was longer and scruffier than it had been when she'd come.

Wonder he isn't already snatched up. Plenty of pretty girls eyeing him at that barn dance. But perhaps, like her, he simply hadn't found the right person. A woman who listened to his poetry and fully appreciate his kind and generous spirit.

He offered his elbow and she took it, following him down a grassy path.

"Looks like the bees are settling pretty well," he said.

"Your father truly loves them," she replied. "That's the best start you can ask for. We've given bees to folks who threw them out in the yard, thinking they wouldn't need a thing. The hives mostly swarmed and flew away or wild animals broke into them to raid the honey."

"That must've made you sad."

"More so angry. Especially Iris. She names most of the queens and she takes it personally when folks don't treat them right."

He tipped back his hat. "You and your sister seem like you have a better relationship than any siblings I've met. Of course, I'm not the most qualified judge since I'm an only child."

"Probably because we're best friends as well," said Fern.

Law's steps were sluggish; his eyes half closed.

"You seem tired," Fern said. "Are you sure you want to go for a walk?"

He shrugged. "I was more thinking of a leisurely stroll. I'd go anywhere, if it's with you."

Though she'd become used to his sweet compliments, the words still warmed her heart. "I'd like to make sure we take Iris to the beach before we go home."

"Definitely," said Law. "Doctor says it'll be another week before Carl can travel, at the very least." He pursed his lips into a thin line. "I don't envy him the trip, poor fellow. Not a fan of strong drink but he might want to have a jug of whiskey along, to tolerate the pain." He chuckled. "Iris's friend Mayor Wiley might be able to get a hold of something like that."

"Don't be calling him a friend around Iris," Fern warned. "Now that we received word from Mother and she knows we're both safe, there's no hurry for us to return. She wouldn't want Carl to suffer any more than needed."

The path wound back behind the house in a direction she hadn't explored before. "Fancy a walk through the forest?" Law gestured to a thick grove. "It's beautiful, especially now at the end of spring."

"Sounds lovely," she replied.

They meandered down a worn path, through the massive cedars. One of Fern's earliest memories was her first encounter with these trees, when they'd hit the great forest in the mountain passes on the Oregon trail.

She tilted her head back to gaze at the far-reaching branches of one behemoth. "We have trees like this on our farm, but nothing this big."

Law nodded. "Probably fifteen, twenty feet across. I'd hate to think of what would happen if it came crashing down."

Flowers burst from every hill and valley, vermilions and

crimsons and purples brightening within patches of green.

"It's like an enchanted wood." Fern plucked a pink blossom and inhaled its fragrance. "So many types of flowers I don't recognize."

"Perhaps because we're close to the ocean." Law stopped beside the largest tree yet.

"Come around the side, I want to show you something." He stepped down a little hill and held out his hand. "Watch out. A bit steep."

Fern grasped his hand, a thrill running through her as their skin touched. Loose stones tumbled down the steep embankment. Good thing she'd worn her most sensible shoes on this trip, any other pair, and she might have turned her ankle. A half-dozen steps and she lit next to him. The ridged surface of the tree rose beside them, and within the trunk a gaping maw, with ancient scorch marks around the edges. To her surprise, the space was large enough for them both to stand inside comfortably, with room to spare.

"I'll check for spiders," Law said as he ducked in.

Fern put her hand on her hip. "I'm not afraid of bugs." She stepped in beside him. Suddenly the realization hit her; they were all alone in the dark, and very close. His breath was heavy around her, and she wondered if he could hear her heart beating.

"This is amazing." The thick bark walls muffled her voice. "Did you create this?"

"Me? Oh no." He chuckled. "I found it as a young boy." He

paused. "Actually, Graham was with me. We figured the Indians burnt it out to make a camping place." He gestured in the semi-darkness. "We found a bunch of arrowheads and pottery shards by the creek."

"You and Graham must have really been good friends." Fern rubbed her arm to rid it of goosebumps. *We're too close. We really should be more careful. People will talk if they find out we spend so much time alone.*

"We were the best of companions." Law's shoulders sagged. "I'd rather not talk about that."

This feud has made such an impact on their lives. Fern couldn't imagine having such unrest between her and a friend. Or her sisters! *Perish the thought.* She touched the long-scorched wood. "I wonder how this tree survived such an act?"

"I'm not sure," Law scratched his chin. "But every year it sprouts new leaves and twigs. So I know it's alive."

"Somehow it has healed." Fern said. "Perhaps your friendship with Graham could heal as well."

A sad smile played on Law's lips. "I hope so." He tugged at her hand, and she followed him out of the tree and into the forest's dappled sunlight. "Fern, I love that about you. Your kind heart and faith in humanity."

He knelt and studied the forest floor. After choosing a small stone from the assortment that covered the ground, he turned it over in his hands. "I feel . . . like you and I have so much to say, but we put it off. At least . . . I have. It almost seems like our hearts speak to each other. Have you felt that way?"

"Sometimes." Warmth crept into Fern's cheeks. "Yes. Often, really."

"I've never experienced that with anyone." Law placed the stone, warmed from his hands, into her palm.

The rose quartz pebble glistened in the sun. Fern's fingers tingled. "No. Not with anyone."

Law stood and paced a few steps away, then swung back to face her. "You'll be gone in two weeks. Suddenly, it seems like the shortest time in the world. We'll blink, and it'll disappear, like dew in the sunshine."

A lump rose in her throat. "Oh, it's so short, Law!"

"Fern, do you think . . ." He took a deep breath. "I'll inherit the ranch someday, of course, but until then . . . I was wondering . . . there's a clearing near this place. The house my father built is still there, nestled like a robin's egg, surrounded by trees. He's given it to me."

"It sounds wonderful." She moved away a few inches. "Wouldn't they miss you at the ranch house?"

"They might." He tilted his head. "But I think we'd want space for ourselves, don't you?"

"We?" she batted her eyelashes, feeling ridiculous and beautiful and wonderful all at the same time.

"Oh, Fern, don't tease." He sagged against the tree. "You're the only woman for me and it will break my heart forever if you don't promise to be my wife." He pulled his long-bladed knife from its sheath and handed it to her, hilt-first. "You might as well stab me through the heart if you don't say yes."

"Goodness, you must be the most dramatic man in God's creation. Take this thing and put it away." She returned the knife and folded her arms. "Most men would hold out a ring, if anything. I suppose I might marry you anyway."

Elation swept over his face, like a sudden gust over resting leaves. "Truly? Oh, Fern." He leaned down, and his lips found hers.

Love and joy and every other bright emotion filled her heart as she returned his kiss, clasping her arms around his neck. But she pulled away quickly and gave him a reproachful glare. "Mister Burke. That is hardly proper, seeing we're not married yet! Why, you haven't even met my mother!"

The joy drained from his face. "Do you think she'll say no? Would you change your mind if she did?"

"Of course not," said Fern. "To both. Mother would consent to me marrying a peg-leg pirate if she thought it would make me happy. But even if she didn't, I'm a grown woman and can choose for myself. I will be sad to leave the farm and my sisters. But sometimes one must leave one glad place to find another."

"White in the moon the long road lies
That leads me from my love."

Law quoted softly.

He dipped his head. "What if I told you everything was ready?"

"You don't mean with the house? I thought it had been abandoned all this time?"

His cheeks reddened a little. "Two years ago, on midsummers' eve, I had a dream. I saw the woman I was to marry, but her back was turned toward me." He drew out Fern's braid, which hung down her back, and moved it over to the front of her shoulder. "But I saw her hair, long and lovely, the color of the deepest honey. The moment I picked you up from that rocky road and held you in my arms, I knew you were that woman. That's why it's been so hard to contain myself."

"That's why you never married?"

He shrugged. "Oh, the biddies tried to play matchmaker. But none of the young ladies were right. Of course, they couldn't be."

He stared off into the trees. "Ever since that dream, I spent what scant free time I've had working on the little house, hoping my love would come along some day. And here you are at last."

Fern wiped away a sudden tear. Law's eyes glimmered with such happiness, and she knew hers must shine the same way. "I can't wait to see it."

He smiled. "I believe it will suit you very well. But . . . can I keep it a surprise for a little longer? Now that we've met, there's a few things I want to change. Of course . . . when we get married, you can fix anything you desire, but I want to try and see if I can get it right."

For some reason, this warmed Fern's heart even more. As the youngest of the family, she'd received hand-me down dresses and dolls most of her life. Rarely had she possessed something created only for her. "I would like to see what you come up with."

"How long?" he studied her face. "How long shall we wait?"

"Not very. But I need time. To speak to my family. To think things through. Can you wait a little while?" she pleaded. "I promise not to torment you for eternity."

He gave a gusty sigh. "I suppose tonight is out of the question." He held up his hands to her reproachful look. "I'm teasing, of course! We've only known each other three weeks. We'll give it some time. But at least I can do this."

Kneeling, he took her hand and pulled a ring from his breast pocket. "This is more appropriate than a knife, wouldn't you say? I've kept this near to my heart for over a year. It gleamed at me from a shop window, and I knew it was for you. Even though I didn't know you." He chuckled and slipped it on her finger.

The warmth of the tiny ring of gold spread through Fern's fingers and into her soul. "Oh," she whispered.

"I simply couldn't wait another moment to see it on your finger," he said. "It's engraved with a verse from Song of Songs."

"I am my beloved and He is mine?"

He nodded. "The Bible has the best poetry of all. Dear Fern, please marry me and make me a better person. Walk with me through the storms and sunshine. Grow old with me in spirit, body and soul. Will you?"

Tears streamed down her cheeks. "Yes, Law. I will."

"Then I'm about to perform another indiscretion." He rose and leaned closer. "Only, we're truly engaged now, so it doesn't matter so much." He kissed her on her nose, her eyelids, and then lightly on her lips. "There. Now it's sealed for all time."

A squirrel scolded them from a branch above their heads and Fern laughed. "Mr. Squirrel, don't you know we're engaged!"

Law laced his fingers through hers and led her back to the ranch house. "Who shall we tell first, Fern of mine? Oh, of course, your sister."

"I'm betting she already knows," said Fern.

12
Teacups and Tempests

Fern untangled the minute thorns from her voluminous skirt, an inch at a time. A hasty step, too close to the path's edge, had caused this incident. Mrs. Crenshaw's daughter had said that with a little one on the way she wouldn't be wearing the simple tea dress any time soon. Fern still didn't want to rend the pink-sprigged fabric.

"Go back whence you came, you wicked dragon." She tossed the branch into the brush.

Mrs. Crenshaw folded her arms. "Can we please hurry? The Dawsons value punctuality above all things and I don't want to receive a scolding from the elder Mrs. Dawson when we arrive."

Iris rolled her eyes. "I'm sure Fern meant to become tangled in the brambles, Mrs. Crenshaw. Besides, if anyone peeps out the window, they'll notice we're here."

"Sorry. I'm ready." Fern brushed a leaf from her stiff white collar and rearranged the dress to drape properly. "Let's go inside."

The house belonging to Ginny White and her new husband was small and squat, with none of the stately grandeur of the homes they'd seen. No decorative gingerbread graced the roof or windows, and the roof over the porch was kept aloft by four rough timbers.

Fern had seen Ginny White in the Burke's church, though they hadn't yet been introduced. She'd seemed a tiny, quiet person, with wisps of blond hair peeping from under her bonnet. Her husband, Archibald Dawson, was quite the opposite. Tall and dark, with a cheerful, booming laugh. When Fern had seen them together, he'd had a protective arm around his wife, as though she were a China doll, fragile and precious.

Mrs. Crenshaw led the way across rounded steppingstones to a modest, whitewashed front door. She knocked.

A thin woman with graying hair and widow's silks ushered them inside. "Mrs. Crenshaw," she said, through pursed lips. "We are pleased you received my daughter-in-law's invitation. Welcome to her tea."

"Mrs. Dawson, may I present Fern and Iris Founder." Mrs. Crenshaw gestured to them.

Fern and Iris bobbed their heads. "Pleased to meet you," they said in unison.

Fern held back a groan. Formalities such as these always irritated her. Why couldn't people use more original speech? *When I'm married, will I be expected to host events like this?* The thought made her cold. *Being married to Law will be worth it*, she reminded herself.

"We are glad to have you," said Mrs. Dawson, wrinkling her nose. Fern wondered if she'd ever been truly glad about anything. *Poor Ginny, having to share her new home with this miserable creature. Everyone has their burden to bear.*

Ladies filled the cramped parlor with rustling skirts and light chatter. Overstuffed chairs and a settee made up the seating arrangements, while China figures, lamps and intricate doilies covered every cabinet and shelf space. Mrs. Crenshaw had informed Fern that most of the decorations had come from Mrs. Dawson's home, with Ginny having precious little say.

I wonder how Ginny likes her new home? She must spend hours dusting. Fern's thoughts turned to the cabin in the woods. How would she like the way Law fixed it up? He said she could change any aspect she desired. *But I wouldn't want to hurt his feelings. We like so many of the same things. I bet I'll love every nook and cranny. And it will be ours.* She clasped her hands and sighed.

Ginny Dawson brought out a porcelain teapot, delicate as the first winter's frost and decorated with ornate golden leaves. She placed it on a table in the center of the room and turned to Fern. "I'm so thrilled you and your sister could come today." Her thin cheeks glowed. "And I hear you're engaged yourself! Isn't it the most wonderful feeling?"

"I'm ecstatic," said Fern. "Though it's a wonder how fast the news has spread. It only happened two days ago."

Ginny laid a slender hand on Fern's arm. "I was so fortunate. Mr. Encritt, the loading master down at the docks, had been trying for my hand, and I'd thought I'd have to give in." She shuddered. "The man is my father's age and has exactly one tooth. But then Archibald came to work at the docks, and he absolutely stole my heart."

"Too bad for Mr. Encritt," Fern murmured.

"Pooh to him." Ginny waved her hand. "All he wanted was a cook and housekeeper. He married a sailor's widow."

"Sounds providential," said Fern. She was glad Ginny chose to share this story with her instead of Iris. Iris had views about women being forced into marriages.

"Mother Dawson, could you please bring in the second teapot?" Ginny said this with such a look of adoration in her eyes that Fern realized her earlier fears had been unfounded. At least, for now, Ginny was happy with her situation. *Better than being married to an old tyrant. But I would absolutely lose my mind. Thank goodness Law and I will have our little house to ourselves.*

Mrs. Crenshaw went around the room for the Founder sister's benefit.

"You've met Miss Portant, Mrs. Collins and Mrs. Lavinia." These women nodded and smiled. "Here are Felicity Martin, Josephine Davis, and Margarite Blight."

These three younger ladies nodded curtly, chestnut, gold and aburn curls bobbing along trim shoulders, with smiles that were anything but warm. Margarite Blight's expression was more of a scowl.

Fern glanced at Iris, who shrugged. Iris was accustomed to being treated coldly by other girls.

However, I will have to live among these people, so I'd better do my best to get along. Fern smiled so brightly her cheeks hurt, until Mrs. Crenshaw raised her eyebrow. She hastily stirred her tea and took a sip.

Mrs. Lavinia nodded to Iris. "I hear your hired hand is doing much better."

"Yes, Carl certainly is," said Iris. "No sepsis and he'll keep his leg, the doctor said. We'll be heading home in ten days, Lord willing."

"Poor dear." Mrs. Collins, who was sitting to Fern's left, patted her hand. "Won't you pine away for your betrothed while you're gone?"

Margarite Blight dropped a spoon on her saucer with a clatter. She murmured an apology and sopped up scattered droplets with a napkin.

Ah hah. She must be one of Law's admirers. I'll try not to be mean about it. Fern gave Mrs. Collins what she hoped looked like a modest smile. "We'll miss each other, but I'll be back within a few months, I'm hoping. In the meantime, I look forward to telling my family the news."

"That's right, your mother doesn't even know!" The elder Mrs. Dawson wrinkled her nose. "The very idea. Well, that's what comes of allowing one's daughter to go into the wild without so much as a woman to chaperone. If you were my child . . ."

Iris's eyes gleamed from the corner she'd tucked herself into. "We're very glad we're . . ."

Fern knew that sentence would end with 'not your daughters' and she hastily cut Iris off. "We're very glad we're here, though it has been from strange circumstances. The Lord works in mysterious ways, wouldn't you say, Mrs. Dawson?"

Mrs. Dawson huffed into her teacup but said nothing.

"And what about Mayor Wiley?" Miss Portant said to Iris. "He seemed interested at the barn dance. Has he come a 'calling?"

"He'd better not," Iris said darkly. "Unless he wants to meet the business end of Mr. Burke's pitchfork."

The ladies broke into a gale of nervous titters, laughing behind fans and teacups.

"Mr. Wiley isn't the best catch, we all agree." Miss Portant looked around the circle, and the other women nodded. "However, dear, as one unmarried woman to another." She leaned closer and said in a low voice. "We have little choice, don't we?"

Iris rose, cheeks flaming. "I have every choice, Miss Portant. I have the choice to live as my own self, not beholding to a man who only marries me for what I can give him. I choose to be unhindered by a ring that would weigh my hands with drudgery to propel a man forward to his own goals. I have every choice. And I would never, ever choose a man like Mayor Wiley. I'd rather die."

She stalked out of the room.

The ladies fell silent, all paying great attention to their handwork or teacups.

Further conversation drifted around Fern, who sipped her tea numbly. She longed to follow Iris, but any fragile chance she had to build relationship with these people would be started today. *Do I care? Should I care?*

On the way home, Iris stared out at the road, biting her lip.

Fern patted her. "I'm sorry things got so heated in there. I don't disagree with what you said, but I must learn to get along with these ladies if I'm going to live here."

Iris pouted. "That may be the case, but most of those women are just awful. I thought that Margarite Blight was going to stab you with her hatpin."

"She must be jealous of me and Law," said Fern. "Maybe she wanted him for herself, or she just wants to be married. She's only seventeen; her time will come."

"I can't imagine deciding to marry at seventeen," said Iris. "Why, I was still sleeping in the barn loft during the summer, then."

Mrs. Crenshaw turned from the front seat where she was driving. "Don't be too quick to judge, girls. Many of these ladies have nothing in their lives but gossip and sorrow. Several have lost children, and Mrs. Dawson buried her husband this year."

"The world is full of tragedy," Iris muttered. "Doesn't mean you have to be odious."

"A soft answer turns away wrath," said Fern.

Iris put her head on Fern's shoulder. "You're right, of course. I don't like people poking at Mother when they haven't met her. And it's hard to imagine you standing up against all those biddies on your own when I leave."

"I guess I'll figure it out somehow." Fern sighed.

"Who said you'll be alone?" Mrs. Crenshaw bristled. "I've handled these women for fourteen years, and may I remind you I'm a widow and a housekeeper."

"We're sorry," said Fern. "I wasn't trying to insult your friends."

Mrs. Crenshaw snorted. "Friends? Very few are my friends. And you're not insulting if it's the truth. However." She turned a steely gaze on the sisters, "I don't want you to say you'll be alone."

"Thank you, Mrs. Crenshaw," said Fern.

"Besides . . ." Iris said so quietly Fern barely heard her. "I don't really have a choice, do I?"

What could she possibly mean by that? Fern decided not to push the matter. She gave Iris a quick hug and remained silent for the rest of the trip home.

As the wagon trundled up the Burke's driveway, Fern waved to Law, who waited by the front porch, rocking from heel to toe in his boots. He pulled his hat off as the wagon came to a stop and nodded at Jerry.

Law helped Fern down from the wagon, then Iris. Jerry gave

Mrs. Crenshaw a hand and then led the horse and wagon back to the barn.

"Missed you," said Law. "Did you enjoy the party?"

"The scones were nice," said Fern.

"Those ladies have their vices, but many of them were friends of my mother," said Law. "I hope they were civil to you."

Iris snorted but said nothing.

"That bad, eh?" Law shook his head. "Well, you don't have to go to any of those events ever again if you don't want to." He took Fern's hands and pulled her closer to him. "You may have anything your heart desires."

Carl hobbled out on the porch, using a walking cane fashioned from a long stick. "Hey there, young lassies!"

Fern waved. "Hi, Carl! So good to see you up and about!"

"Shoot, I could run to town if the doc would let me," said Carl.

Fern giggled at the picture of Carl racing to town, the giant plaster cast winking in the sun.

"May I have a moment with you?" Law said softly.

"Of course," said Fern. "Where shall we go?"

"This way." Law gestured to the path they'd walked a few days before.

Iris sniffed. "I suppose I'll have lunch by myself."

"I promise I won't keep your sister for long," said Law. "And after lunch, we'll go to the beach like I promised. Besides, you've had twenty-one years with her."

"Fine, fine." Iris waved them away. "I'll change into something more appropriate for the beach."

Fern and Law meandered down the path, swinging their clasped hands between them like two children.

Law walked past the hollowed tree where he'd proposed. The path joined a much larger trail, wide enough for a wagon.

"Are you . . . are you showing me my house?" Fern gasped. "I thought you wanted to wait until I returned for the wedding!"

Law stroked her cheek. "I couldn't bear the wait, so I added a few small touches while you were at the party. Besides, if there's anything you want to change, I'd need time to fix it up before September. September!" he groaned. "What an eternally long time!"

"Don't fret, my love." Fern took his hand and kissed the work-worn palm. "Summers are busy. The time will fly by, and I'll write to you."

"I'll write you." Law wiped a tear from his cheek. "Stacks of poetry. Every day."

"I'll look forward to it," said Fern.

Trees thickened overhead, and patches of moss that dotted the ground grew denser. Trunks of massive trees that had snapped in storms long ago rose around them, large enough to hold small cottages.

"It truly is like fairyland." Fern clasped her hands.

A fence created from twisted saplings, the sort one would expect to see around a wise-woman's hovel in a storybook, appeared through the trees.

Law tugged on a small gate, which swung open with ease.

"Lady, your home awaits."

The cabin was tiny compared to the ranch house, with walls constructed of thick logs. Two polished windows, one on either side of the little green door, shone like welcoming eyes.

Law opened the door. "Please come in."

Fern stepped into the home.

To one side, a fire crackled in a little hearth made from stones. The mantlepiece was an oddly shaped log, with curious knots and knobs sticking out from the side, but the top was polished smooth as a river rock.

"Driftwood." Law patted the top. "My father brought it in from the beach and spent many winter nights carving the top."

Indeed, most of the cabin held whispers of the ocean. The roughly hewn table and chairs seemed made of the same stuff as the mantlepiece. Seashells of all types and sizes studded the walls of the clay fireplace. White muslin curtains hung on the windows. An assortment of whittled boats and seabirds, along with more seashells, covered the sills.

"Maybe ten minutes to dust," Fern murmured.

"What was that?" asked Law.

"Oh, nothing," she gave him a quick smile.

"Here's our stove," Law gestured to the far corner, where a rather modern cast iron implement squatted. Pots and pans of all sizes and shapes hung from pegs in the wall, and cupboards promised to provide other items of necessity.

"So, what do you think?" Law's eyes held that pleading look Fern was coming to know so well."

"It's perfect," she said. "I wouldn't change a thing."

"Our bedroom is through there." Law pointed to a side door. "But . . . I'd like to keep that a surprise for now."

"I have my grandmother's quilt," said Fern. "And curtains. I have a whole chest of things at home. My glory box, Mother always called it."

"I can't wait to see what you bring," said Law. "Filling our home with your hopes will make it complete."

13
Stormy Weather

Iris perched in the highest branches of the giant oak tree, watching the sky. Clouds hung in thick, dark clumps, and gentle breezes that had caressed her cheeks this morning were changing into gusts.

She and Fern had planned to leave at daybreak, but a storm would make for dangerous travelling. During the springtime, there was no telling when a squall of this sort would roll away.

The week had waned long. With Fern mooning over Law, she'd had many meandering hours to herself. The beach had proven interesting, but she'd decided she preferred the shaded woods to the salt-tinged coast. Every holey sock had been found and mended, and the ranch house glistened from wall to wall. Mrs. Crenshaw tolerated her help for a time, and then she'd shoo her out to 'get some sunshine."

Iris closed her eyes, dreaming of home. Mother would welcome the help they'd bring with open arms.

She longed for her own hives, but Myrtle and Peony knew the basics, and they would care for the bees tenderly. She missed her queens and the workers and was anxious to see if the hives had made use of the unusually good crop of Pendergrass flowers that grew in abundance around their home.

Bees have cared for their own for centuries before humans began to farm them. They'll be fine.

The thought that continued to stand above all others was the eventual loss of Fern. She'd push this down, like rising bread with too much proofing, but it continued to come up. She was happy for her sister, but to know she'd be living a three day's ride away . . . It twisted at her gut.

I wonder if she knows she's my best friend? A lump rose in her throat. She picked a young oak leaf from a twig and watched as it spun down to the forest floor on its own mad journey.

Then there was the unfinished matter of Graham Timmis. She hadn't seen him since they'd parted at the dance after her fit of temper. Perhaps they'd always have contention if they continued to spend time together. But a piece of her, the mischievous bit of her soul, couldn't care less. *Might be worth the turmoil.*

Graham's a busy man, and prideful. If he wanted to see her again, he'd have attempted to do so. *Best to go home and leave it alone.*

A flurry of movement through the leaves caught her eye, and she stepped out on the limb, steadying herself with one hand and parting the branches with the other.

A collection of twigs, twisted together and adorned with feathers, were nestled in a forked branch.

Three tiny beaks poked out of the nest in response to the movement. They gaped open in a silent plea for food.

"Ohh." The babies were so perfect, still blind and pink. *If only folks could trust God for provision the way these baby birds trust their mama.*

Another gust swept through the forest, tossing the limb like a galleon at sea. "Glad your mama made that nest secure," Iris muttered to the baby birds. "I'd best climb down."

As she descended through the staggered branches, a pang hit her soul. More than anything, she wanted to be a mother. She'd never shared this longing with anyone, and in the last few years she'd all but given up on it. The choices for suitable grooms were in low supply, at least around Cottage Grove. And many folks would consider twenty-three past marrying age.

Wistful dreams, all of them. She'd teach the children about bees and riding. *Maybe even how to climb trees.*

The prayers she'd sent up about the subject had been answered by a strange silence. Mother always said, "Sometimes God gives us answers a piece at a time. We are human after all, and the full sight of his glorious plan might blind us if we beheld it all at once."

Iris certainly didn't want to be blinded. *I'd like to have at least a hint.*

A curious path, barely detectable, twisted away from the tree through masses of blue monkshood. She picked through the bushes and saplings partially covering it, searching for bees.

Moisture from the impending storm cooled her skin, and hair whipped around her face in a smoky haze. She tied it up and continued. *I'll only go a short way. I'll have plenty of time to get back before the real storm hits.*

Carefully, she picked her way down the trail, wishing she'd brought shoes.

Fox gloves rose through patches of sunlight in scarlet spires, and evergreen violets glowed in the mossy shadows.

"There you are," she whispered to a tiny, black and yellow striped creature crawling into a violet. "You'd best be getting back before the wind blows too hard for you to fly. I suppose you can find shelter in a hollow log or tree."

She rose, almost bashing her head on the thick split-log fence that divided the Burke and Timmis property line.

A shrill whinny split the air. Iris darted to the fence and peered through the slats, trying to see the horse, but the undergrowth was too heavy. She hiked up her skirts and climbed over the rails.

The path on the other side was in even worse shape. Twigs and thorns reached for her clothes and rocks dug into her feet, though the worst of the stickers were avoided due to soles toughened by years of barefoot excursions.

Another whinny rang through the woods, long and loud. *Something's wrong. Why would one of Graham's horses be all the way back here? It must be hurt.*

Rain began to fall in round full drops that spattered Iris's face and hair. She ignored them and pushed through the thick brush.

The trees thinned, and she came to a clearing.

A beautiful bay mare stood in the center, sides heaving. She raised her head to wiffle the air, her eyes rolling back as she spotted Iris.

"I'm not coming any closer, girl," Iris promised. "Not until I see what's happened."

The mare whinnied again. A tiny, muffled whicker answered back.

"Oh, I see." Iris's gaze flicked over the thicket. "Where's your baby?"

The mare snorted and pawed the ground. She tossed her head and trotted to the clearing's edge.

Iris moved past the mare, giving her a wide berth. The tiny squeals, plaintive and urgent, continued. She followed the sounds to a ravine nearby, carved out by springtime rains. The trench was wide and deep, and through the brush she could make out a thin ribbon stream, sure to rise if the downpour continued.

Iris wiped rain from her eyes and crept along the sides. "Where are you, little one?"

There. A foal, darker than its mama and almost too tiny to believe, struggled in the mud beside the stream. It strained and floundered, trying to stand on spindly legs.

The mare pushed alongside Iris, almost shoving her down the embankment. She whinnied again, right in Iris's ear.

"All right girl, calm down." Iris patted the trembling neck. Though the mare wore a standard halter, Iris couldn't find anything to tie her with. "Please, don't go over the side," she begged the horse. "I'll get your baby. I promise."

The rain pelted fast and cold, rushing down the ravine's slope in a muddy cascade.

Iris slid down the bank, gripping random rocks with her toes to slow her ascent. A twig tore at her exposed hand, and a sharp stump dug into her side as she went past, but she ignored these trivial injuries as she reached the bottom of the ravine.

The horse whinnied again, and Iris craned her neck to meet her anxious gaze. "I'm hurrying, calm down!"

The foal stood to shaky feet as she reached it.

"You poor thing, all covered in mud." Iris used her already soaked apron to wipe away the worst of the muck covering its face and haunches. "No breaks as far as I can see, praise God. Can't tell if you're a colt or a filly with all this mud, but we'll figure that out later."

The remnants of an umbilical cord dangled from the small belly. "Goodness, you're new. Mama must've come out in the woods to give birth and then you got too excited trying out your legs."

Though tiny for even a new baby, the foal was still quite large and gangly. Iris put one arm under its haunches and one under its chin. She hefted it off the ground. The foal must have sensed she was trying to help, or it was simply weary from the mucky ordeal.

Whatever reason, it settled in her arms.

Staggering to the edge of the ravine with her cumbersome burden, she eyed the foreboding slope, where the trickle of rain had become quite a torrent.

Her feet stuck in the bog with each step, and the ache in her side from earlier intensified. She pressed her hand to where the stump had ripped her dress and drew it away, sticky with blood. *Wonderful. God, please don't let it be too serious.*

Sinking down on a boulder, she cuddled the shivering baby in her arms. "I don't know how we're going to do this, Stormy. I can't leave you here. But I can't stay in this rain, either." With desperate eyes, she searched the sides of the ravine for an alcove or cave. Any kind of shelter from the continuous deluge. *But if we stay too low, we could be swept away.* A dam could break upstream at any time, releasing a deadly flood.

The foal tucked its head on her shoulder, its tiny breaths warming her ear. A faint pulse beat against her arm.

"Come over this way," a voice hollered. "There's an easier trail."

She staggered to her feet, hope warming her soul.

Graham emerged through the curtain of water, peering down from the top of the ravine several lengths away, the mare poking her head out beside him. He gestured to her. "It's hard to see in this rain," he shouted, "But come this way."

Iris's shoulders sagged. *Thank you, thank you, thank you, God.* "I'll try!" she yelled to Graham.

"Let's see if you can walk," Iris told the foal as she set it down. She draped her arm around its neck and tugged in the direction Graham had indicated. "Come on, let's get out of here."

To her immense relief, the foal wobbled alongside her with no sign of injury. Her side burned, but she ignored the pain and pressed forward.

Around the bend, there was indeed a better path in the rocks, slippery, but much more plausible than the way she'd come down.

Graham was already halfway down the slope. "Get him up here!" he yelled. "There's an anchor sapling I can grip!"

Despite the circumstances, her heart danced a little jig at the sight of his handsome face.

She pushed and pulled the shivering foal up the slippery slope to a boulder that jutted out to make a solid resting point. "Pretty heavy for such a little thing," she gasped.

"If you can get him up a few more feet I can help," said Graham. "I'm worried if I go down too far, I'll slip all the way down the hill. Then where would we be?"

"I agree." Iris gripped the foal's neck and haunches. With a mighty heave, she pushed it up to the next shelf in the rocks.

"Fortunate he's so new." Graham slid down the slope, closer to the foal. "Another few days and he'd be putting up much more of a fight." With one hand still gripping the stout sapling, he slid his arm under the foal's front legs. He tugged while Iris pushed, trying to avoid the tiny, scrambling hooves.

Finally, he hauled the foal over the last ledge.

Rain dripped from the rim of Graham's hat, a normal broad-brimmed one instead of the fancy bowler he'd worn when she'd first met him. The look suited him much better.

He took a deep breath, then reached for her hand, gripping hard to keep her from slipping away.

"I can manage," she said, "Mind the foal."

"I don't want to lose you either." He pulled her hand. More rocks and roots tore at her dress and bare toes as she clambered up to join him.

They leaned on the rocks, gasping.

The mare crashed through the bushes and charged over to her baby. She glared at Iris while she checked it over.

"The thanks I get for saving your child." Iris chuckled.

The foal stood and began to wiffle along the mare's side.

"I know you're hungry," said Graham, "But we need to get you out of this rain."

He stood and reached a hand to Iris. "And you."

As she rose, she pressed her palm to her injured side.

"Wait. Is that blood?" Graham pulled her hand away, frowning.

"I don't think it's serious," Iris said through chattering teeth.

"No way to know until we look at it." Graham tilted his head. "We have quite a hike back to the house, but there's an old shack close by. Let's try to get to shelter and then we'll see."

"All right."

Graham gathered the foal in his arms, and Iris followed him

through the forest.

The mare crashed after them, her anxious nickers trumpeting through the storm.

Mud covered Iris from head to toe, and her dress clung to her body. Hair stuck to her cheeks in wet strands, and she gathered her skirts over one arm, heedless of her lace-trimmed pantaloons peeping from beneath.

Graham huffed and puffed, the foal's legs almost dragging on the ground. "This fellow may look tiny, but I'd bet he weighs seventy-five pounds," he said. "I'm amazed you got him up that ravine."

"Not the first foal I've had to carry," said Iris.

"I imagine," he said, grinning back at her. "Your face was covered in pure determination when you ascended that hill."

He sat the foal down and pointed through the trees. "See there? That's the shed. We'll do fine there until this rain stops pelting."

14
A Talk with Graham

A sagging paddock surrounded the building, which was constructed from logs and sported a bark roof. Despite the apparent age of the edifice, Iris had no doubt the little hut would make a reasonable shelter. *Anything is better than this rain.*

Iris unlatched the wide door and shoved it open across the many years' accumulation of dirt and leaves.

Must and dust filled her senses as she stepped inside. Only the faintest of light shone through a tiny window near the roof of the building, situated under the eaves so as not to let in the rain. She hoped an errant snake hadn't taken residence in a dark corner.

Graham carried in the foal and placed it on the floor. The mare pushed through the door, giving anxious nickers.

"Here you are," said Graham, patting her neck. "You and your baby can rest now."

He walked across the barn, groaning as he stumbled over something in the dark. "There's a shelf . . . I think there's a lantern and flint somewhere . . . ah, yes." Sparks fluttered in the semi-darkness, and then a flame. Light bounced around the walls.

Graham checked the floor along the far corner. "Come this way, little fellow." He gave the foal a gentle nudge. "You and your mama can rest here."

The mare squeezed in beside her baby and snorted.

A large wooden chest rested in another corner. Graham lifted the lid, sending a cloud of dust and hay into the air. He knelt to study the contents. "My grandfather was a member of one of the first parties to venture down the Oregon trail. A mountain man, who even worked as a trail scout for a while. Had one too many encounters with the Sioux and became a bit paranoid, even though this area hadn't seen a hostile native for years. Built this little shed and outfitted it for an emergency Indian attack. He'd bring me out here when I was a boy and show me all the supplies, just in case. I send a hand out to refresh the items and check for critters once a year."

He picked up an ancient musket. "I forgot this was in here. This thing was old when Grandfather built this place. Must be a hundred now. I ought to take it up to the house and clean off the rust. Probably wouldn't fire without taking someone's head off, but it would be nice to put it on display."

"It's nice you found it," Iris replied, attempting to sound interested, though her current freezing state made it difficult to lend the proper amount of enthusiasm to her tone.

"My goodness, what am I thinking?" Graham turned up the lantern's wick and held it closer to her face. "'Those beautiful lips are turning blue." He returned to the chest and pulled out a bundle. "Here's a few blankets. These might be a bit musty, but not too bad, since I've had them replaced recently. You ought to get warmed up before we hike back." Spreading them out, he checked them over. "No sign of mice, that's a wonder."

She took a blanket. "Thank you."

"Hang on. Before you wrap up, let me see that wound," said Graham. "I have a handkerchief in my pocket. rather soggy, but clean, at least."

Iris had forgotten about the throbbing in her side, but she obediently moved her hand and shifted to the light.

"I'm afraid we'll have to throw propriety out for the moment," said Graham.

"It's all right, I trust you." As Iris uttered these words, she realized they were true.

Graham pulled the ragged edges of cloth away from the wound and gently cleaned it.

Iris bit her lip but couldn't hold back a wince.

"Seems I keep hurting you, though I'd rather shoot a hole in my head," muttered Graham.

"I'll be fine," said Iris, closing her eyes.

"It doesn't look deep," Graham said finally. "You'll need to clean it better when this storm passes, but I think you'll live."

Rising, he went to the door and held the handkerchief in the rain, wrung it out in a thin red stream, then cleaned his hands. He returned and pulled the blanket over her, tucking it around her shoulders. "Now try to rest."

As Iris snuggled into the blanket, the rain on the roof turned into something much harder, as though dozens of children were hurling rocks at the shed.

"That's hail." Graham sighed. "It'll be a while before we can head to warmth and comfort, I'm afraid."

"I'm cozier than you'd think," Iris said. "I only hope Fern doesn't worry about me too much. She probably thinks I ran to the barn. That's what I usually do back home with these sudden storms."

"You're shivering. Here." He shifted

She obediently moved closer, and he put his arm around her. "Not that it's much help, since I'm fairly soaked myself." He chuckled. "Blast it! I wish we could start a fire, but this old place would ignite faster than matchsticks."

"This is nice," she said, putting her head on his shoulder, scandalous though it was. *He's preventing my death from the cold*, she reminded herself. Even the most puritanical town woman couldn't object to that.

The foal found its mother's teat and slurped greedily, its little brushy tail wagging.

"Stormy," Iris murmured.

"What's that?" Graham shifted in his place and stared down at her.

"Wouldn't that make a nice name? And it would suit a colt or filly."

"Oh, I didn't tell you?" said Graham. "He's a colt. Jolly little fellow, too. Last of his bloodline. His father was the finest stallion I've ever owned. Died last winter." He pulled her closer. "Iris's Storm. And we'll call him Stormy for short."

Silence engulfed the room, only punctuated by the pelting hail. The drowsiness that comes from heroically saving horses, being drenched, and being so close to Graham's beating heart finally began to affect Iris's senses, and she fought to stay awake.

"I felt badly, you know, at the dance," Graham blurted. "The mayor gets my ire up. The morning contest didn't help either. But I shouldn't have allowed him to spoil our evening." He closed his eyes. "I wanted to call on you every day. Aunt Corrianne gave me fits about it. I wanted to apologize, and I was uncertain when you'd be heading home." He removed his hat and raked his hair back with his fingers. "I'm so sorry for my disgraceful actions. The thought of never seeing you again has been almost unbearable. But . . ."

"Law." Iris folded her arms. "Did you hear about my sister's betrothal?"

"I had a feeling it would come to that," Graham groaned. "No mistaking the look in his eye."

Iris rested her hand on his arm. "Why do you hate him so much?"

A muscle in his cheek tightened. "Surely you know the reason by now."

"Something about a fire?" Though Iris knew the story, she needed to hear it from his own lips.

Graham rose and paced across the packed dirt floor. "We lost three of our finest brood mares that night. Have you heard the sound a horse makes while it burns to death?" He covered his face with his hands. "I'll never forget the screaming. Offences towards me I can tolerate; but tormenting innocent creatures . . . I won't forgive that. Ever."

"Can you consider the matter rationally?" Iris held out her hands. "Why would he save your life if he hated you so much?"

Graham clenched his fists. "He didn't want to hang for murder, that's why. Might have hung anyway, if they'd had enough evidence. But they couldn't convict him for merely living next door, though I had witnesses who'd seen him threatening me the previous week."

"Boyish utterings, Graham," Iris insisted. "Did you ever say things you didn't mean at that age? Perhaps even in the same conversation, I'd wager."

Graham lowered his eyes. "Perhaps. But I didn't burn down his barn."

"Oh, he didn't burn down your barn either." Iris rose and took his hand. "I've seen the way Law treats his horses, his dog. Even his chickens. I can't imagine even the darkest of boyhood anger compelling him to hurt any living thing. Has he ever done anything destructive to a living soul while you've known him?"

He stared at her, eyes widening. "No," he said finally.

"Bitterness is a festering wound, isn't it? Wouldn't healing be a relief?"

Graham rested his head against the doorframe. "Yes."

"I believe that's why Jesus talks about mercy and forgiveness so much," said Iris. "Forgiveness is a key that frees us from the most dark and dreary places. Jesus forgave the most terrible wrongs ever committed against a human."

He looked back at her, tears glimmering in the corners of his eyes.

"I've read the same verses, and I've heard God speak these things to my heart," he murmured. "But it's been so long. I don't know how to let go."

Iris rested her hand on his arm. "You must let God do it for you. We don't possess the power to do these things on our own."

He gave her a quick smile and wiped his tears away with the back of his hand, looking so boyish that Iris longed to take him in her arms and stroke his hair.

"Surely you realize Law didn't do that terrible thing," Iris ventured, her heart thudding in her chest.

"I don't know." He straightened, and the man returned. "I will pray about the matter."

Iris fell silent and huddled by the wall. After years of working with farm hands, she'd learned a few words could do more than many, and a seed, once planted, needed time to grow.

Soon the hail quieted, and only a gentle rain pattered on the roof. Graham stuck his head out the door.

"Looks like we can make it back to the house. We'd better go straight to the Burke's so they won't fret and you can get into dry clothes." He waved to the now peaceful mare and colt. "There's nothing that will harm them here. I'll get Henry to bring out water and hay. They can stay here for the night."

He held out his hand, and she took it.

"I'm so glad Stormy is safe. What a beautiful little colt," Iris said.

"Yes." Graham led her through the door. "Thank you for saving him." He raised an eyebrow. "What were you doing out in the forest anyway?"

"Climbing a tree."

He chuckled and shook his head. "Why does that not surprise me in the least?"

They walked back through the light drizzle. The beautiful flowers lay broken and dead on the forest floor in tragic splendor. Hailstones dotted the ground, some bigger than a man's fist. Graham picked one up. "I don't remember ever seeing such hail. I hope it hasn't damaged our house or stables."

"I hope the bees are alright," said Iris. "Mr. Burke's hives are quite sturdy, so I'm sure they'll be fine." What about the baby birds? She hoped their mama covered them in time.

Graham pursed his lips. "Hopefully so. The mare was missing when I put the herd up for the storm. That's why I came out here to look for her."

"I'm glad you did," said Iris. "Can't imagine trying to get that foal up the ridge on my own."

"Yes, but you were going to try." His eyes glinted.

"Of course I would have. I promised the mare." Her teeth were chattering again.

His brow furrowed. "How about I send a man over to the Burke's house to tell them what's happened? I'd bet Fern'll send you over a fresh change of clothes. Then you can get all cozied up to the fire in one of our guest rooms and have something hot to drink. Twenty more minutes in this state and you'll catch your death."

"I-I think that's for the best," she stammered.

They reached the manor's back porch. "Come on in and I'll speak to my aunt, let her know what's happened," said Graham. He opened the door and glanced back. "Goodness, I never thought you could be more beautiful than you were at the dance, but here you are."

She gave a short laugh. "Whatever do you mean? I must look like a wet cat. I'll be surprised if your aunt allows me through the door."

"You're more beautiful because you're not angry at me anymore and everything is all right." He took her hands. "Isn't it, dear Iris?"

She dipped her head. "I'm not angry anymore. As for anything else . . . we shall see."

15
Danger in the Dust

The hooves of the Burke's old carthorse clattered on cobblestones as the wagon rolled into town. Iris retied the bow of her borrowed hat, suppressing the urge to throw it into the street like she'd once done with a pair of church shoes as a child.

Fern sniffed. "Told you that bonnet would drive you crazy." She patted the thin ribbon of her simple sunbonnet with a superior, sisterly air.

Iris rolled her eyes. "Keeps my skin from burning. Last thing I want to deal with on the ride home is a painful sunburn. And I couldn't very well wear that battered man's hat I brought with me."

Mrs. Crenshaw slapped the reins across the cart horse's broad back. "It's going to be quiet without you two around the house." She gave Fern a wink. "But I suppose at least one of you won't be away for long. A wedding will be real nice."

"Are you sure you'll be happy to have another woman around?" Fern gave a teasing smile.

"Goodness yes!" Mrs. Crenshaw grinned. "Someone who won't track mud through the house and can carry on a womanly conversation? It'll be downright refreshing."

Iris rested her chin on folded hands. Since the foal and storm incident, Graham had called on her twice, and actually been civil to Law. His intentions were obvious, but she couldn't see a future for them without a reconciliation between the two men. They needed time, and right now, her time was running out.

Mrs. Crenshaw drove the wagon up to the hitching post on a side street behind the bank and the general store. "We'll get a few things for your return journey. Most of the supplies you'll need are at the ranch, but we can still have a look-see." She patted Fern's hand. "Besides, you must take a peek at the lace old man Lantry received in the last shipment from Boston. T'would make a lovely veil for a certain bride-to-be."

"Of course, I'd love to." Fern gave Iris a disparaging look. Several women had stopped by from town with wedding ideas, including Miss Portant, who'd offered her grandmother's ancient, moth-eaten dress.

Fern had confided she didn't want to decide anything until she could consult with their mother, Peony, and Myrtle.

Mrs. Crenshaw climbed out of the wagon, and Fern and Iris followed.

As the housekeeper tied the horse to a hitching block, she paused. "Ooh, I almost forgot! I'd better stop by the bank and withdraw a few dollars. Time to square up Mr. Burke's credit at the store. Wouldn't want the old man to be upset with me. You two want to join me?"

"I'll sit in the wagon," said Iris.

"I'll come along," said Fern. "The sun is already high and hot."

"You won't find the inside of the bank much cooler," said Mrs. Crenshaw, "but suit yourself." She bustled off in the direction of the bank building.

Fern began to follow.

Iris's throat tightened. She snatched Fern's hand. "Wait. Let me go."

"What is it?" Fern whispered.

"I don't know." Iris's thoughts raced, and she ran a hand over her eyes. "It might be nothing, but . . . please stay out here. I'll go with Mrs. Crenshaw."

Fern shrugged. "All right. At least the wagon's in the shade."

Mrs. Crenshaw glanced back. "Are you coming dear?"

"Yes ma'am," said Iris.

True to the housekeeper's word, the bank was stuffy and dark, with nothing for light except for three small windows and a few lamps burning on countertops.

Mrs. Crenshaw swept up grandly to the counter. "Yoo-hoo, Mr. Hollister? Are you here?"

Shuffling sounds echoed through the room, and an elderly man appeared from a side door. He grabbed a monocle hanging from a chain on his faded waistcoat and held it to his eye. "Why hello, Mrs. Crenshaw. In need of money today?" He peered over at Iris. "Oh, is this one of the young ladies who's been staying with you?"

"Yes, indeed." Mrs. Crenshaw gestured to Iris. "Meet Iris Founder. Her sister, Fern, is betrothed to Master Law."

A pang hit Iris's heart. *I really must get used to being introduced as the sister of the bride.* She gave a tight-lipped smile. *Lord, please help me give you this situation and be happy for my sister.*

"You don't say?" Mr. Hollister's monocle popped from its place and he scrambled to put it back. "Well, it's terribly nice to meet you, Miss Founder. Now Mrs. Crenshaw, what can I get for you today?"

"I need five dollars, please, from Mr. Burke's account, to settle my credit with Mr. Landrey. I was so distracted by the new gloves at his establishment last week that I forgot to pay him."

Mr. Hollister tsked and shook his head. "Oh, we can't have that, Mrs. Crenshaw. You know how upset he gets. Wait right here and I'll fetch the money from the safe."

He shuffled through the side door, his tufts of white hair bouncing up and down.

Mrs. Crenshaw opened her reticule and checked through the contents. "Oh, where did I put my spectacles? Did I leave them at home?"

The bank door banged open, and she started, almost dropping her handbag.

Two men stomped inside, slamming the door behind them. Thick cloths covered both of their faces from the nose down.

Iris tried not to stare.

The first man swaggered up to the counter. His hair scraggled down his shoulders in greasy strings and he smelled like a pig's trough. "S'cuze us, ladies. We have business with the banker here."

Iris froze. She'd heard that voice before, and recently. A moonlit night . . . the sound of meat frying over a fire . . . *Sir, can you spare a nickel?*

Metal glinted in the lamp light as the second man drew a small revolver from under his filthy shirt and pointed it at Iris. A tremor ran through her body, as though he'd already shot her.

Mr. Hollister stood in the doorway, his jaw hanging open, bills clutched in one fist. "Wh-what's going on here?" he stammered.

The first man gave an exaggerated bow. "Excuse our manners, asking to be helped before these lovely ladies and all, but under the circumstances, I'm sure they won't mind. Mister banker, would you give us whatever gold and money you have in that safe back there?"

Mrs. Crenshaw whirled around, her eyes lighting on the gun. She covered her mouth with a gloved hand. "Land sakes."

The first bandit gestured with the gun. "Why don't you two

women go sit over there against that wall where you can't get into any mischief?"

Mrs. Crenshaw shrank away, staring at the gun. "I don't know. I don't . . ."

Iris grabbed her shoulders. "Let's go, dear. Everything will be fine."

"I, what am I supposed to do?" Mrs. Crenshaw spoke as though in a trance.

Sweat pooled on Iris's forehead, and her knees wobbled. "Dear Mrs. Crenshaw, trust me. Let's go sit down."

"I mean now!" The bandit with the gun strode forward and slapped Mrs. Crenshaw's wrinkled cheek.

"Ahhh!" Mrs. Crenshaw bent down, cupping her cheek with a gloved hand. A crimson mark glowed beneath her fingers.

"How dare you!" Iris cried. "We'll do as you say: there's no need to hurt her!"

She took Mrs. Crenshaw's hand and dragged her across the room. "Come on, let's sit right here."

To her supreme relief, the older woman sank down. Iris joined her on the wooden-planked floor.

Mrs. Crenshaw laid her head on Iris's shoulder, squeezing her eyes shut. "Lord have mercy on us all," she moaned.

The second man's bandanna covered his expression, but Iris could still see a gloat in his glittery, cold eyes. "That's right. Womenfolk should do as they're told."

Iris glared at him, seething. Her little pistol sat heavy in her handbag, hidden beneath her skirts. *They'd never expect it. But these men are clumsy and stupid. I can't risk someone getting hurt.*

The first man reached over the counter and grabbed Mr. Hollister's elbow. "Now Mister banker, it's not going to take much to make us happy. Everyone can go home without no bullet holes in their skins today. Just hop on back to your safe and fill up these gunny sacks." He threw a bundle at Mr. Hollister's face.

Mr. Hollister stared at the man, unblinking.

"You heard me!" the man barked. He cocked his gun. "Get going or I'm gonna start shootin."

"No need for that," Iris spoke up. "I'm sure Mr. Hollister heard fine. Didn't you, Mr. Hollister?"

The elderly man snapped out of his trance. "Yes. Yes I did. I'll get the money right away."

The older man pulled his own gun from a holster and followed Mr. Hollister to the back, while the younger man gestured to Iris and Mrs. Crenshaw. "You two scootch away from the door. That far corner should do nicely." He went to the door and slid the bolt closed with sickening finality.

Iris tugged Mrs. Crenshaw's hand. "Let's go over here."

They crawled to the corner, globs of dust clinging to their skirts.

Mrs. Crenshaw sneezed. "Place has gone to ruin since Mrs. Hollister passed," she whispered.

Iris closed her eyes. *The things people think about.* But her own thoughts tumbled over themselves in mad dashes to be heard.

Stories of bank robberies and stage hold-ups were told far and wide, each one more sensational than the other. But she never imagined she'd be in the middle of such a situation.

Mrs. Crenshaw shuddered, and Iris squeezed her hand. "Pray," she said in her ear. The elderly woman's eyelids fluttered closed, and she bowed her head.

Iris sent up a silent prayer of her own. *God, please deliver us. Please help me to know what to do.*

The doorknob rattled.

The younger robber leapt to attention. "Harvey, did you hear that?"

"Yeah." Harvey came out of the back, bulging sacks swinging from both hands. "Probably just another old woman coming to get money. They'll give up when they can't get in."

Fern. Iris sent up a silent prayer *S*he *knows we're here. Probably saw the men come in too. Please let her go for help.* A sudden thought warmed her soul. *Perhaps she's already gone. Someone will be here to rescue us at any moment.*

"Watch them." Harvey went to the window and pushed back the curtain with the tip of his gun. "Yeah, whoever it was must've given up. Don't see no one out in the street. Hmm." He stepped back, surveying the room. "Barney, what are we going to do with these folks? Don't want them chasin' after us." He nodded at Iris. "Especially this little spitfire here."

"We could lock 'em up in the vault," Barney suggested.

"They have air in there?" Harvey asked. "Don't want no blood on our hands."

"Eh, they'll be fine," said Barney.

Iris wondered at the competency of robbers who hadn't planned what to do with witnesses. She remembered a saying of Carl's. "A dangerous man with half a wit is twice as dangerous as a man with a whole one. Can't predict 'em."

Ms. Crenshaw trembled so hard from her place against Iris that she shook them both.

A memory flashed into Iris's mind. As a little girl, she'd fallen into a river, swollen from melted snows. She'd struggled and screamed, fighting the current, until she was almost too numb to move. With her last ounce of strength, she'd grabbed an old, frayed rope floating in the water. It happened to be tied to a tree on the bank, and she'd managed to pull herself to safety. For years she'd thought of that rope, forgotten by man, but placed there by God for the needed time. *God, you knew this would happen here, today, and you've already created a plan. Please deliver us.*

16
Plans

A thumping noise startled Fern from her reverie. She'd been reading one of Law's poetry books for a good fifteen minutes. The magical words had swept her away in their cadence, and she'd paid little attention to passersby.

A farmer banged on the bank's door with a gloved fist. "What in creation? Mr. Hollister, it ain't fourth of July for two months!" The farmer spit out a chaw of tobacco. He shook his head and walked away, muttering.

Fern laid her book aside and squinted at the sun. How long had Mrs. Crenshaw and Iris been in the bank, anyway? Surely enough time to fetch a few dollars. And why wasn't the door open for the farmer? Iris and Mrs. Crenshaw had walked right in. *That's what I get for not paying attention. Perhaps they came out, went on to the store and the banker locked up afterwards. But Mrs. Crenshaw was pretty set about showing me that fabric. Why wouldn't they have stopped for me?*

She slid from her perch on the wagon seat and approached the bank building slowly. Something warned her not to try the door. Instead, she crept through the brush and bushes that grew up against the faded white building. She inched her way to the window, keeping her head low and away from the glass.

A man's gruff voice drifted through a tiny crack in the window frame.

"You folks get in that room now, you hear? Except for the pretty one. You're going to stay right here with me and my rifle."

Fern clamped a hand over her mouth, and tears sprang to her eyes. *How could those men have gone in without me noticing? Me and my scatterbrain!*

She fumbled for a tiny dagger she always wore at her side. *I'll come through the window. Maybe if I catch them by surprise.*

Her fingers froze on the thin bone handle. *No telling how many are in there, or if they have guns. Impatience will only lead to trouble.* And it always did, where she was concerned. She slid down against the wall, rough wood digging into her back through her dress.

God, give me wisdom.

A familiar bowler hat bobbed over the bushes a short distance away, and she sat up straight, a little hitch in her throat. Not her first choice of rescue, considering the chilly way he still treated Law when he'd come to see Iris, but someone was better than no one.

"Graham!" she hissed.

The hat moved further down the street.

She crawled out of the bushes, then leapt up and sped past the building as quickly as she dared.

"Graham!" she called.

He pivoted, and she stopped short to keep from plowing him over. As it was, his hands landed on her shoulders, and he stared down into her face. "What's the matter, Fern?"

She collected her thoughts like a pile of unraveled yarn. "Graham, the bank . . . bandits . . . Iris and Mrs. Crenshaw . . ."

His eyes narrowed. "Are you sure? Iris is in there?"

She nodded. "I'm positive."

"My gun's in the coach." He swiveled on his heel, but he shook his head. "We need more people. Hurry." He turned and ran down the street.

She followed him to the sheriff's office, where a man was pounding a nail into a loose slat.

He tipped his hat as they approached. "Morning."

"Deputy Baron, there's trouble," Graham said gravely. "We've got bandits in the bank."

The deputy dropped his hammer and bounded to them, sweat pouring down his round, red face. "You don't say? That's no good. Especially considerin' Sherriff Alder's an hour away, visiting his lady friend." His eyes shifted to the bank building. "Think they're armed?"

"I overheard them say so through the wall," said Fern. The

adrenalin that had built up within her was dying down. Her legs felt as wobbly as a newborn colt's.

"Hang on." The deputy ran into the building. He returned with two muskets, handing one to Graham. "I can't deputize you, but I can give you this."

Graham checked the sites. "Thank you. Hopefully, we won't have to use them."

Fern longed for a gun of her own but realized arguing with the deputy would take more precious time. "Let's hurry, please."

They rushed down the street. The deputy frequently removed his hat to mop the sweat from his shining bald head. He huffed and puffed as he ran.

Graham gave him a slanted look and then raised an eyebrow at Fern.

Yes, I wish the sheriff was here. Her faith in the deputy was thin.

Mayor Wiley stepped off the boardwalk as they approached the bank, squinting at Graham. "Deputy, what are you doing with these folks?" His gaze shifted to the muskets. "And why the guns?"

"Bandits at the bank," the deputy said hoarsely. "Armed, Mayor."

"I thought I saw a couple of old nags I didn't recognize." The mayor pulled out a cigarette and lit it with a match from a box in his coat pocket. "We'll gather more men with guns and storm the door. Deputy, I'll lead the front attack, and you come in from the back."

Graham stared at him. "That's the most foolish notion I've heard this week," he hissed. "We need to stop this yelling and get off the street, out of sight. We can't storm the building. The men have hostages. Come over this way." He ducked behind a shed.

Fern followed, and they were soon joined by the deputy and a scowling Mayor Wiley.

"I'm not a coward." Mayor Wiley folded his arms. "I don't skulk behind buildings when there's a fight to be had."

Deputy Baron pursed his thick lips. "No, Graham's right. We must think carefully and make the best plan. Otherwise, innocent people could get hurt, either when we barge in or when the bandits come out. Let's think about this." He rubbed his chin. "Most of the men folks are down at the docks today. New shipment came in from the east."

Fern stared out at the building, wishing one of the walls would fall away and she could see what was happening. *Iris, be careful!*

Another man approached the bank building. Fern's heart gave a little flutter. *Law! What's he doing in town?* He'd been clearing out a pasture all morning, and evidence of his work covered his clothes.

Graham leaned his head against the building and groaned. "What a day."

"Law, over here!" Fern whispered as loud as she dared.

Law's head swiveled, and his eyes widened. He ducked behind the shed and took Fern's hands. "Darling, why are you hiding here?" He glanced at the three men. "Deputy? Mayor? Graham?"

"Seems we have a problem with bandits," the deputy drawled. "And your housekeeper and this here girl's sister is stuck in with 'em."

Law clutched the knife in his belt. "We have to rescue them, of course."

"The bandits have guns," Graham said. "If you have any brilliant ideas we're here to listen."

"Since no one agrees to the better plan of rushing the building, I'd say we pick 'em off as they come out," said Mayor Wiley. "I've won ribbons at the fair for best shot." He winked at Fern. "Wait 'til you see how fast I shoot 'em. Won't know what hit 'em."

"No one is taking potshots at anyone," said Law. "You could kill an innocent person." He gestured to a woman strolling down the street with her little girl.

Impatience prickled Fern's mind. "We must do something soon. What if they decide to kill or hurt my sister? Or Mrs. Crenshaw? Or the banker?"

"I believe the decision is being made for us," the deputy said gravely.

The door to the bank inched open, cracking wider and wider. Iris and Mrs. Crenshaw stepped out together, and Fern exhaled. *Could I have imagined it? Perhaps I heard wrong.*

Graham started forward but stopped just before he reached the line of visibility.

Fern's blood ran cold when she caught sight of a rough leather glove tightening around her sister's arm. A man, his face covered by a bandanna, followed the women through the door.

"No," Graham whispered.

Law grabbed Fern's hand and squeezed. Warmth flooded through her. At least she didn't have to endure this terrible moment alone.

Iris's eyes flashed over the square, and she stared at the wagon where the Burke's horse still stood patiently. Hope flickered over her face.

She's wondering where I am. Fern shifted her position, willing the feeling back into her feet. *She's hoping I realized something was wrong.*

As the group neared the hiding spot, cold steel glinted in the sunlight behind Iris's back.

Bile rose in Fern's throat. *My sister could die. At any moment, that clumsy oaf's finger could slip . . .*

Her fingers clenched into fists, and she stepped out from behind the building. The deputy yanked her back, his face like a thundercloud.

Anger reverberated through her being, though she knew she'd been foolhardy. *How can he possibly understand? That's my big sister. She pulled me down the Oregon Trail with her seven-year-old hands and watched over me my entire life.*

Iris and Mrs. Crenshaw stumbled down the bank's steps, their skirts covered in dust and dirt. Tears streaked Mrs. Crenshaw's face, and a red handprint covered one withered cheek.

A second man, also holding a shotgun, paused and scanned the street.

Mayor Wiley sucked in a breath. "Two," he muttered.

"Might be more waiting inside," Graham said.

The bandit moved down the street towards the little party hiding behind the shed. He pushed Iris. Mrs. Crenshaw hobbled in front of the second man.

Iris stared ahead, eyes burning in defiance. She walked stiffly; chin held high. The first man kicked the back of her leg, and she stumbled forward, almost falling.

"I'll kill them," Graham muttered. He lifted his musket.

Law pulled him back. "Wait. We must wait for the right time."

Two farmers walked towards the bandits and the two women, deep in conversation. As the group approached, the farmers stopped in their tracks.

"Yeah, yer eyes ain't fooling ya," yelled the first bandit. "I do have a gun trained on this innocent woman's back. And I'll keep it there until we're safely out of town. You fellas weren't interested in getting this purty young lady kilt, were ya?"

"I hear gettin' back shot is an awful way to die," the other man put in. "Our fingers are mighty itchy right now."

"So you two just scoot off the path over there." The first man jerked his head to the side. "Afore I consider taking me another hostage or two."

One farmer spat at the bandits, but they both slid off the road like wary dogs watching a bear.

The second bandit looked over at the building where Fern, Graham, Mayor Ingram, and the deputy were hiding. "And don't think we didn't notice you all over there." He gestured with his gun. Come on out, I'd like to have a conversation."

"Do they have any idea who they're dealing with?" growled Mayor Ingram. "I'm tired of listening to you fools." Before anyone could stop him, he stepped out into the open, pistol leveled at his waist.

"You crooks get your hands in the air where I can see them!" he shouted.

"Have it your way!" the first bandit screamed. "This woman will die!"

"You're going to get everyone killed!" Law darted out in front of the mayor, grabbing at his gun.

A shot cracked through the street.

Fern heard someone shrieking, a high, terrible keening that seemed to reach to the very heavens. She realized it was her own voice.

Red droplets flecked the mayor's crisp, white shirt, and Law staggered and fell to the dirt.

People scattered. Iris snatched one of the bandit's muskets and whacked him over the head with it. He crumpled to the ground.

The other bandit threw Mrs. Crenshaw to the side like a rag doll and high-tailed it down the road.

The Deputy, Mayor Ingram, and the farmers ran after the bandit.

Fern rushed to Law and sank down by his side as blood ran out into the street.

17
A Crack in the Door

Iris stood at the large picture window in the ranch house parlor. The sun was sinking, and all that remained was a tiny golden sliver, like a crack in the doorway of a secret world.

Fern came in from the kitchen, drying her hands on her apron. Her face was thinner, and her eyes held an older look, like she'd aged ten years in the last three days.

"How is he this afternoon?" Iris asked.

Fern dipped her head. "Feverish, still. Doctor said we were lucky the bullet went clean through. Would have been much worse if he'd had to go fishing for it."

Iris shuddered. "I can't bear the thought. That bullet could have easily hit me or Mrs. Crenshaw."

"But it didn't." Fern gave a weak smile.

Iris patted her shoulder. "I'm sorry this has been such a hard time for you."

"If only the fever would break!" Fern cried. "I wish . . . I only wish . . ." her chin trembled.

Iris put her arms around her. "What do you wish?"

Fern's shoulders shook, and she buried her face on Iris's shoulder. "I only wish Mother was here. I miss her so much and she would know what to do. I'm glad you're with me," she added. "But I wish Mother wasn't so far away. And I've realized this is how it will always be. When I'm married."

"Oh, Fern." Iris said, stroking her hair. "Don't forget, you'll be with the man you love. Things will change. But you will have a new beauty in your life."

"But what if the fever doesn't go away?" Fern's wails grew louder.

Iris held her close for a long time until the gulping sobs turned into sniffles. At this point anything she said about God's mercy or healing power would be something Fern already knew and would bring little added comfort.

Finally, Fern tipped her head back. "I'm sorry," she gasped. "I couldn't stop."

"You haven't cried in days," said Iris. "I think you've saved it all for now."

Fern took a deep, shuddering breath and clutched at her apron. "I could lose him! I could lose him forever!"

"Goodness. Let's go to the kitchen and get you a cup of tea."

Iris steered her back through the door and led her to the table. "Sit right here."

Fern obediently sank into a chair.

Iris went to the stove for the kettle that always waited on the back. Mrs. Crenshaw was fond of random tea breaks during the day and firmly believed the beverage could cure all ailments. She poured a steaming cup and handed it to Fern.

The two sisters sipped tea in silence for a few moments.

Iris studied Fern's face over the rim of her cup. She couldn't imagine the state of her sister's heart. *Law will be fine . . . but what if he isn't?* The thoughts went over and over in her own mind, like a never-ending loop. She closed her eyes. *Lord, I must give this to you. It's so far out of my control.*

When she opened her eyes again, Fern was staring at her. "Anything?"

Iris shook her head. "Not this time, Fern. I'm sorry. But I know God is faithful, and he works all things together according to his purpose."

Fern sighed. "I know." She stirred her tea in endless, aimless circles. "Would you mind terribly . . . if I . . ."

"You need a little time to yourself?" Iris rose from her chair. "Of course I don't mind."

She glanced out the window. Only a few moments of daylight remained, but she rose and headed for the little door that led outside from the kitchen. "Be back to check on you shortly, Fern."

Sugar cubes were kept in a box on the shelf, and Iris grabbed a handful and stuffed them in her pocket. She slipped on a pair of wooden clogs that sat by the door and went outside.

Violet streaked the sky like paint from a Master artist's brush. An owl hooted from a nearby tree, a wild, yearning sound that sent pangs to Iris's heart. *I long for things too, Mr. Owl. I hope you find your heart's desire, be it a meal or a Missus.*

She wandered through the woods, soaking in the coolness of twilight and the hush brought on by evening. Bees no longer buzzed, and the calls of day birds were silenced. *God, it's always good to walk with you.*

A fence rose before her, the now-familiar divider between the Burke and Timmis property. Without hesitation, she climbed over and continued down the forest path. Past the clearing where she'd found the mare, and past the shed where she'd weathered the storm with Graham and the horses.

Stepping out from the thicket into the long, far pasture, she walked through the grass, keeping an eye out for clumps of horse manure and snakes.

The stables were a stretch away, grouped together like a watchful band of friends. An occasional whinny sounded through the night as Graham's prized horses said goodnight to each other.

Iris stopped at the paddock fence and rested her chin on the top bar.

Some horses had already gone into the stable for the evening, but not little Stormy. He bounced around his mother on dancing hooves.

She held out the sugar and Stormy's mother came over to take them from her hand.

Stormy came beside his mother, sniffing for his share. Little sprigs of mane stuck out in every direction like a black bristle brush. His white star gleamed in the twilight.

"You don't get sugar yet," Iris told him.

"He's turning into a beauty," Graham said behind her. "But he's a little rogue. His mother doesn't quite know what to do with him."

Iris turned. "Sorry to come so late. You did say I could visit at any time."

"I meant what I said." Graham's smile was soft. He took her hands, and a thrill ran down her spine.

"Oh Iris, I've wanted to come and see you, but I didn't want to intrude with Law in danger. The nights I've spent on my knees!" He took out a handkerchief and wiped his forehead. "Is there any change? Perhaps you came to tell me?"

Her face must have given the answer. He put a hand to his eyes and looked away. "He must get well, Iris. For so many reasons, but most of mine are selfish. I couldn't bear him to leave this earth without me telling him . . ."

Hope rushed through Iris's soul. "You mean . . . you forgive him?"

"How could I refuse?" Graham clutched at his hair until it stood wildly on end. "After such a noble act, to throw himself in front of a bullet to save you. While I stood there like a dolt."

"Don't give yourself a hard time about that," Iris smoothed his rumpled collar. "No one knows how they will react in a sudden crisis."

"You were also quite heroic," Graham said. "Hitting that bandit over the head with his own gun."

Iris shuddered. "I didn't feel brave. Both horrible men are in jail, that's what counts."

Graham paced along the fence line. "I'm glad. But the whole incident has made me realize, of course, everyone else was right all along. Such a brave and kind man could never have tortured innocent creatures. Or hurt me."

"I only wish Mayor Wiley had been thrown in jail with the other vagrants," Iris said bitterly.

"You haven't heard?" Graham's face lightened. "Folks decided that after the shooting, such an unstable man couldn't continue to be mayor. They rallied at the courthouse and demanded he step down. He left town in disgrace."

Iris sighed. "At least he won't bother me anymore."

Graham stiffened. 'He wouldn't bother you any way."

Boots clomped towards them, and Graham's coachman waved from the other side of the fence. "Ho, there."

Graham released Iris's hand. "I'd better see what he needs."

"And I'd better return to the house to check on Fern," said Iris.

"Best hurry, it's almost dark," said Graham.

"I'll be all right. I have a few more moments," she said.

Graham strode away, turning once to look behind him.

Iris's lips burned with unspoken words. She headed back through the woods.

When she returned to the kitchen, Fern was still at the table where she'd left her.

She glanced up at Iris. "Hello. You've seen Graham, haven't you?"

Iris nodded dumbly.

"And?" said Fern.

"And . . . he's forgiven Law, so that's good."

Fern took a sip of her tea, saying nothing.

Mrs. Crenshaw came into the room. "Hello, dears." Her own eyes were red and moist.

"How is he?" Iris hardly dared to ask.

"Law is at peace."

Iris's heart sank to her boots. "You don't mean . . . is he?"

Fern dropped the teacup, and it shattered on the table in a cloud of ivory shards.

"Oh my goodness, no!" Mrs. Crenshaw ran to Fern and hugged her. "His fever is broken, darling! He's sleeping now."

Fern stared at the puddle of tea and broken China. "I've ruined your cup," she whispered.

Mrs. Crenshaw wiped a tear from Fern's cheek. "Oh, my poor dear, don't worry about it. My own fault for my fumbling words! I've hardly known how to speak these last few days. Please forgive me."

"Iris, did you hear that?" Wonder filled Fern's voice. "The

fever has broken."

Iris squeezed her hand. "It's wonderful. Here, let me help you clean this up."

Together they stacked the bigger broken pieces in a pile and sopped up the tea.

"Let me get the dustbin," said Iris.

Mrs. Crenshaw lifted the lid from a large pot that hung over the fireplace. "Soup's ready. Would you like to see if Law's awake, Fern? You can take him some." She ladled soup into a bowl and placed it on a tray with a spoon.

"Better let me," said Iris.

"No," Fern rose. "I want to. I feel much better."

"All right," said Iris.

Fern took the tray and padded away

Iris poured herself another cup of tea.

"All's well that ends well," said Mrs. Crenshaw.

"Thank the Lord," said Iris.

Fern hesitated outside the door, listening for gentle breaths to let her know if Law was awake or not. *I'll just set the soup down beside his bed if he's asleep. He needs his rest, poor man.*

She pushed the door open a crack, still listening.

"Please come in." The voice was weak and strained, but unmistakable.

Every time she'd gone into this room the past few days, she'd had to prepare herself for the flushed face, the rolling eyes that couldn't focus, the slurred words and sometimes even lack of recognition. But today, the face that met her gaze was that of the man she loved so well. White and drawn, but so much better.

"Hello, beautiful," Law said.

"Oh, Law!" Fern reminded her feet to take slow, unhurried steps, and forced her hands to still and place the soup down in a calm manner. *Don't squeeze him to death. He's been shot.* She mollified herself by giving his hand a gentle pat. "How are you, my darling?"

"Hungry," he said. "I suppose that's a good sign."

"It certainly is!" The times they'd tried to feed him in the last few days had been difficult. He'd spit out the food and sometimes sworn at them. Mrs. Crenshaw had been horrified, exclaiming she didn't know he knew such words, but the doctor had told them it was all because of the fever.

Now she held out a spoonful of the bean soup, and he took the bite.

He closed his eyes. "Now if that isn't the best soup I've ever eaten Served by the prettiest hand that ever held a spoon."

Fern giggled. "Just eat your soup and get better."

18
Farewell

A somber group gathered around the wagon as Fern, Iris, and Carl prepared for the journey home.

"Do you have enough to eat?" Mrs. Crenshaw asked, darting a glance at the back of the wagon.

Iris studied the bags of food and supplies the housekeeper had been loading all morning. "I can't see why not. We'll barely fit ourselves."

Fern stood to the side of the wagon; her brown braid nestled against Law's neck. Her shoulders shook with sobs, and he bent low, whispering in her ear.

Poetry, most likely. Iris rolled her eyes. *For Pete's sake, we're returning in two months to prepare for the wedding, and I'm sure he'll find an excuse to come to Cottage Grove before then.* Even as Iris thought this, she felt a pang of envy. *At least Fern has someone who cares enough about her to say goodbye.*

Her neck hurt from craning to check the driveway, and her eyes stung from the strain. She hadn't seen Graham since that night at the horse stables. He'd sent word that he'd been called away, but the messenger didn't say why. Perhaps a quality horse had come up for sale.

She folded her arms. His livelihood was important. *But surely he could say goodbye?* His voice had dripped in fear when he'd talked about the danger she'd been in. When they'd talked at the stables, she'd felt she'd meant something to him. *As much as he means to me.*

Now Carl was calling in a gentle tone. "Come, Fern, we want as many miles before the sun hits peak as possible dear. Don't forget, I'm old, and tired."

Fern moved away from Law, but he pulled her back and kissed her soundly on the lips. "Don't forget me, my love," he said.

"Why in the world would she forget you?" said Mrs. Crenshaw. "If she couldn't remember you in two short months, I'd worry about her being addled in the brain."

Fern wiped tears from her cheeks. "I'm coming, Carl," she said.

Law stepped up to Carl. "Take care of my girl," he said gruffly.

"Don't you worry, none." Carl patted the musket at his side. "My leg might be healin' still, but there's nothing wrong with my trigger finger."

"Not to mention that us girls have our own weapons, and we're both crack shots," said Iris. "Come on, Fern."

Fern climbed up into the back of the wagon to sit beside Iris, arranging her skirts. "Let's go," she said to Carl.

Carl slapped the reins on the broad, velvety backs and the wagon creaked forward.

The goodbye party grew smaller and smaller, until the handkerchiefs they waved resembled fluttering moths.

Iris couldn't help but stare down the road towards the Timmis ranch as they rumbled further and further away.

"I'm sorry," Fern said in a low voice.

"Sorry about what?" Iris replied, far too brightly.

"That Graham didn't come to see you off." Fern glanced down. "I know you care for him, perhaps even as much as I care for Law."

Iris's chin trembled, and she grew furious at its betrayal. "I don't know if anyone could care for a man as much as you care for Law, could they?"

Fern hugged her knees, her skirts all bunched up around her. "I'm sure they could, and I'm sure they do. But I am terribly happy, Iris. We will be married by the sea. And you and Peony and Myrtle shall be my bridesmaids." She clasped Iris's hand. "If you will."

"It would be my greatest honor." Iris smiled. It was hard to be sad with her sister's infectious joy radiating around her. And the fact remained. They could be attending a funeral, rather than planning a wedding.

Of course, there was much to be determined. How would the farm spare the five Founder women for the weeks they'd be gone? Would Granny decide to brave the two-day journey in the rumbling wagon? If not, who would care for her?

Does he even think of me? Iris's shoulders sagged, and she leaned against a trunk, allowing herself to fall into a deep hole of sorrow. *Just for a little while. Then I'll climb out and try not to think of it again.*

Evening settled over the little hill as the wagon rumbled through the final mile towards the farm. Happiness bounded into Fern's soul, mixed with the strange, sweet sorrow her heart had only known for the last few days of their journey; the sadness of being separated from the man she loved.

Her family must come and meet Law before the wedding. Her sisters would want to be bridesmaids. And a part of her needed time to tromp through childhood haunts and bid them farewell.

"Don't worry, my darling," Law had said. "Our little home needs a final touch or two. We'll go to our own places to prepare and meet up again at the beginning of fall for the most beautiful little seashore wedding the world has ever seen."

Now that home was in sight, Fern was even more grateful she had returned, even for a little while.

They stopped at the gate, and Iris jumped down to open it. Their golden dog, Barney, loped up the driveway, his tongue hanging out of the side of his mouth.

Tears filled Fern's eyes, and she shook her head. *If the mere sight of that silly dog makes me feel this way, I'm not going to be able to hold it together when I see Mother.*

Iris opened the gate, clasped her hands, and exhaled. "It's wonderful to be home."

"Amen," said Carl from where he rested in the back of the wagon. Sweat beaded his forehead. He hadn't complained much, but Fern could tell the journey had been long and painful for him, and she was glad he'd finally be able to return to his little cottage where he could rest and finish healing.

Iris waved her past. "I'm going to run home on foot with Barney."

Fern clucked to the horses, and they ambled down the driveway, while Iris disappeared into the trees like a willowy dryad.

I wish Graham would have pulled himself together. I want Iris to feel the same happiness I'm experiencing. And since I AM marrying Law, it would be wonderful to have Iris live next door forever.

Familiar trees rose on either side of the road, waving gentle branches.

There it was. Home. Peony and Myrtle flew from the door like giant butterflies, swooping in as the wagon came to a stop.

There was much embracing and exclaiming. Iris joined them, out of breath.

Mother looked into each face and nodded to herself, as though assured that all was right, all was as it should be. "Girls, you are different," she said.

"I can still smell the sea in your hair!" said Myrtle.

"We washed it at the boarding house." Iris laughed.

"Still," said Myrtle.

Granny whacked her cane against the post from her seat in the ancient porch rocker.

"Sorry, Granny, of course we missed you too!" Fern trooped up the porch steps and hugged the bony stooped shoulders. She patted the gray cat, who was almost always in her lap. "Hello, Edward."

Granny peered into her face. "So you survived your gallivanting, eh?" she said. "I always said no woman should have to ramble more than a mile from her home, it's far more trouble than it's worth."

"It must have been extra trouble to come all the way down the Oregon Trail from Boston, Grandma," said Iris.

"You'd better believe it." Grandma jutted out her chin and picked up her knitting needles.

"We must go inside so you can open your presents!" said Fern. "Let's get our carpet bags in so I can find them."

The ladies worked together to get Carl settled in his home and unload the wagon. After a delightful supper of roasted chicken and green beans, the women settled around the fire in their favorite chairs.

Fern and Iris handed out the trinkets and the shells they'd collected for all.

Fern pulled a brown, spiky shell from her bag. "This one is a hairy triton." She handed it to Granny. "If you hold it to your ear, you can hear the ocean."

Granny did as she was told but frowned. "All I hear is a bit of swirlin' and shufflin," she complained.

"That's pretty much what the waves sound like, Granny," said Iris. She gave Mother a starfish the size of a man's hand. "I found this fellow on the shore. He was all dried out, but there are live ones everywhere. Purple, yellow, and pink like this one."

"Imagine that!" said Mother. She placed the starfish on the center of the mantlepiece. "You never know what you'll find on adventures."

"Even husbands," said Peony.

Fern blushed and picked at a stray thread on the quilt that covered the chair where she reclined.

"So this Law fellow wants to take you away from us?" Myrtle said in a teasing voice, though there was a hint of regret in her tone.

A lump formed in Fern's throat. "Well, I wouldn't go if he wasn't just the most wonderful man in the entire world."

"Bound to happen one of these years," Granny croaked from her chair. "Can't expect four beautiful women to stay homebodies forever, that's what I always told your mother."

"Of course not." Mrs. Founder poked at the fire and frowned. "I always knew this time would come, and I would be wrong to advise you differently. Your letters mentioned many things about Law I truly liked. He is respectful, a hard worker, kind, and . . . "A twinkle sparked in her eye. "There's poetry."

"Poetry?" Peony said. "You can't be serious, Mother!"

Mrs. Founder nodded gravely. "Oh, but I am."

Fern opened her mouth in protest, but Iris spoke before she could. "Don't worry, ladies, he's not a sissy. He is a good man, and he will care for Fern . . . if she needs caring for. She has chosen well."

"Thank you, Iris." Fern rose. "And now I think I'll go to bed. My head still throbs sometimes, and the journey has it smarting." Her forehead truly did ache, but it had also become a nice excuse to remove herself from awkward conversations. She couldn't remember a time when she didn't want to talk with her family, but tonight she longed for Law, and this conversation had her fighting back tears.

So many changes. But they are good changes. Needed changes. Law's smiling face rose in her mind, and she hugged herself. *Soon, I will belong to him. I can't imagine life any other way.*

###

That night, Fern awoke in her little loft bed. Her head ached still, and she rose to find a cool cloth to soothe it.

As she came back up the stairs, she heard stifled sobs coming from the bunk beside her.

"Oh, Iris," she whispered. "You must be hurting dreadfully."

"He's such a silly man," Iris said scornfully through her tears. "With his top hat and his carriage. Why did I have to fall in love with such a silly man?"

Fern patted her hand, marveling at the strangeness of playing advisor to the sister she usually turned to for wisdom.

"You obviously see other things you love about him," Fern said in a low tone.

"Yes." Iris wiped her eyes with a corner of the worn quilt. "Might be hard to see at first, but Graham is full of passion and discernment. He understands my relationship with God more than anyone outside of this family, and he also loves God with his whole heart, though he's had to work through much pain and bitterness. I could envision him as a father to my children. But . . ." her face crumpled. "He must not see me that way, Fern, or he would have spoken to me. Somehow, he would have sent word." She covered her face with her hands. "How could I be so wrong? I was certain!" Her voice dropped to a whisper. "Oh, how can I bear it?"

Fern's throat tightened. There was nothing she could say to comfort her sister. For she could not fathom, in any capacity, the desolation she would feel if she were in her place.

19
Resolution

Iris placed the cover over the final beehive and peered at the tiny bees gathered at the entrance, their legs bulging with pollen sacs.

"Good evening, ladies," she whispered. "We'll be harvesting your treasure soon, but I promise we'll leave plenty for you and your children."

She moved through the hives, shedding her veil and gloves. The supper bell had rung ten minutes before, but the tree branches rustled, beckoning.

Her feet, sure as always, carried her to the old apple tree. She placed her supplies in a little pile on a stump and swung up into the first branch.

Normally, when she climbed, more troubles would slide off her shoulders the higher she ascended. But today her heart remained heavy, and sadness still clung to her skin like sweat.

"I must move past this," she whispered fiercely. "It's been four weeks and no word."

Law would be here soon. He'd vowed to visit every month at least, as ranch work permitted. But in his many letters to Fern, he'd said nothing about Graham. *Graham promised to tell him he'd forgiven him. Wouldn't Law at least mention that? It's not like he worried for fear of wasted ink, with the reams of poetry he's sent.*

Iris plucked a leaf from its twig and twisted it absent mindedly. *I wonder if Fern will really wait until the fall to be married. Would I wait? It would be so tempting to gallop away with my love on his horse the moment he came.*

Why torment herself with such thoughts? *The life of a spinster is my destiny.*

The instant this thought filled her mind, it was countered by the Voice she knew so well. *Patience, my daughter.*

"I've been here long enough. Time to go home," she spoke, to whom, she wasn't sure. *Maybe the tree.* She patted the rough bark and prepared to step down to a lower limb.

The branches crashed beneath her, and for a moment she wondered if a bear was trying to climb after her.

Don't be silly. The dog would have raised an absolute ruckus.

"Fern is that you?" she called. "Be careful. You still get headaches when you climb. Give me a minute. I'll come down to you."

"I'd appreciate that." Graham's head, thankfully bare of his hat, appeared through the branches.

Her stomach flipped. "What on earth? How did you ever?" she stammered.

"How do you do this all the time?" he puffed.

"Years of practice," she replied, trying to stifle a giggle and press down her heart, which had almost leapt from her chest, at the same time. "Here, give me a moment."

She swung nimbly to the lower branches. Goosebumps covered her skin. *Am I awake? Is this really happening?*

Graham landed hard. He stood, brushed off leaves and twigs, and took her hand as she slid down the last stretch of trunk.

She fell into his arms. When she tried to step away, his grip tightened.

"Oh no. I have ridden two days to see you, with a second madman who was also missing his ladylove. I've endured countless stanzas and verses of meandering poetry recited to me in the most forlorn manner you could possibly imagine. Would you indulge my fancy and allow me to look at you for a moment?"

"I suppose I could do that," she murmured.

"Ah, Iris. I've missed you." He smiled down at her, his eyes glinting with the sweet tenderness she'd seen that first night after shedding her disguise at the supper table. "I only hoped . . . you would forgive me for not coming sooner."

"I did wonder," she said, trying to keep her voice level.

He stepped away and rubbed his chin. "Remember when my groom was gesturing to me at the stables? He'd come to tell me a dear family friend, Raymond Alburg, whom I well respected and owed a great deal, was dying. Jerry brought news that Law had improved. I chose to leave for another town without delay."

"Oh." Iris sank down on a flattened stump. "I'm sorry to hear that."

"I made it to his deathbed in time to thank him, for that I was grateful. Then I helped to settle the estate." Graham spread out his hands. "His situation was quite complex, with livestock and properties to manage. His widow knew nothing of the business, so it took quite some time."

"I would say," Iris mumbled.

"Aunt Corrianne kept pressing me to let her send word. But I wanted to tell you myself. I stubbornly kept thinking, surely tomorrow I'll have this finished." His forehead furrowed. "But there were so many tomorrows, Iris. All I could think about was you, and how I'd missed saying goodbye . . . and so many other things that needed saying. I was in absolute agony."

"I see," she said coldly. *Can't he know the torment I've been through?*

"When I returned a week ago, I talked to Law. We settled everything. He was gracious enough to forgive all. He told me he was coming. I begged him to allow me to accompany him on the journey."

"And here you are." Iris lifted her chin. Now the initial shock had worn off, she felt as though, despite having good reason, he should be punished for treating her so, if only just a little. "How did you get here? In your fancy coach?"

He bowed his head. "No, I came on horseback. I remember someone telling me the roads here wouldn't serve it well." He raised an eyebrow. "Besides, horseback was faster."

His repentant gaze was enough to melt her heart into a puddle, and it took every drop of resolution in her soul to keep from throwing herself into his arms. But she held back.

"How did Law do, with his shoulder?"

"Fine, fine. Fellow's tough as old boots." Graham studied her face.

"Glad to hear it." She picked up her bee equipment. "I'm sure you're hungry. I know I am. Did you hear the dinner bell? I must have missed it. Surely, it's rung by now."

Iris set off towards the house, with the satisfaction of hearing Graham crash through the brush behind her. She refused to look back, even when a muted exclamation alerted her that he must have become tangled in the underbrush.

When she arrived at home, she put away her supplies as normal and went into the house.

The women were already standing at their places, with two extra chairs added to the table. Law stood beside Fern, his hair wetted and smoothed down. He gave her a broad smile. "And there's my third sister-to-be. How are you, Iris?"

"I suppose I'm fine," she said.

Graham appeared at the door, and everyone's heads swiveled as he came in. He gave a tiny bow and went to his appointed seat, beside Granny and quite a way from Iris, in silence.

After the prayer, everyone sat and began passing the food.

"How is Mr. Burke?" Mrs. Founder asked as she gave Law a heaping bowl of mashed potatoes.

"Doing quite well," said Law. "When I see him. I think he might build himself a little hovel and live with the bees, he spends so much time there."

"And the bank bandits?" asked Peony. "What of them?"

"Sent off to prison in California," said Law, as he heaped mashed potatoes on his plate.

"Good," said Iris.

"Boy, why aren't you eating?" Granny screeched to Graham. "Our vittles not good enough for you?"

Graham reddened. "I'm sorry, I don't seem to have much of— um, thank you," he said, as Granny ladled a giant spoonful of beans on his plate and topped it off with the biggest biscuit on the platter.

"No one's starving on my watch," said Granny.

Fern darted Iris a look, but Iris shook her head. Fern went back to buttering her biscuit.

"Mrs. Crenshaw and I found a lovely place for the wedding," said Law. "That is of course, if it meets your approval, Fern. Plenty of room for everyone to stand, and there's a little natural window in the rocks to shelter from the worst of the wind. It's a beautiful place."

"It sounds wonderful, Law," said Fern. She beamed around the table. "I can't wait for all of you to see the ocean."

"I've seen the ocean," said Granny dryly. "In Massachusetts when I was a girl. Don't need to see it again." She turned to Graham, who was manfully choking down the beans. "Don't make me go to the ocean, boy."

Graham looked up with glazed eyes. "I can assure you, I would never dream of doing such a thing."

Myrtle patted Granny's wrinkled hand. "Carl's going to stay here with you, Granny. No one's forcing you to go anywhere."

"Better not," said Granny darkly.

Graham rose from his chair. "Ladies, I am terribly sorry for the rudeness, but I believe the long days of travel are catching up with me and my legs need stretching. Thank you for the delicious . . . beans. I'll return shortly."

He walked out of the room. The front door slammed.

Everyone stared at each other across the table in an awkward silence.

"Poor man," said Peony. "Iris, what did you do to him?"

"I don't know what you mean," said Iris primly. *What about how he treated me?*

"Iris, you know I don't often insert myself into your affairs," said Mrs. Founder, "But in this case . . ."

"For Heaven's sake, girl, go after him!" Granny yelled.

Iris gazed into the eyes of her hopeful family members. Law gave her a wink. "He really is sorry," he said. "I had to hear about it for two whole days. Such mooning you've never imagined."

Iris pushed her chair back and went out the door, amid cheers and clapping. Her cheeks burned. *Will I ever be allowed to mind my own business again?*

She went out on the porch and stared down the driveway. The old retriever's tail waved like a flag several hundred yards away. Graham walked beside him, shoulders hunched, looking sixty years old.

"Graham, wait," she called.

Graham turned, and hope sprang into his eyes. "It's you."

"Yes, it's me." She caught up with him.

"May I?" he took her hand, gently. "Oh, Iris, please! Don't torture me further. Let me speak my heart. I've already done so many things badly. Let me try to get something right."

Iris's skin prickled at his touch, and her determination crumbled. "I'm listening."

Graham stepped back and tucked his hands in his pockets. "What happened outside of the bank . . . it was like in the Bible, where Paul talks about seeing in a mirror dimly. It was as though the mirror was wiped clean suddenly, and I could see everything clearly, like you said. Iris, how could I have been such a fool?"

Iris reached out trembling fingers and smoothed the lines that had formed on his forehead, leaving a small smudge of tree sap. "You allowed hate and bitterness to run through you. It's like the bees. If they don't clean their hive the instant mold or rot begins to set in, it will take over and ruin their home. They eventually die."

"Don't you see? My heart was so dry and withered." Graham clutched at his chest. "It took some time to bring me back."

"God can do anything," said Iris."

Graham nodded. "Iris, you are the most amazing woman I've ever met. So focused on beautiful, simple things of God, without a care for the worldliness of fashion, and decorum, and the petty thoughts of other people. Your beauty glows from within you like an ember."

He took her hand. "I don't know how I could be worthy of you, but I hope someday that I can be."

Any words that sprang into her mind dissipated before they could reach her lips. Everything inside of her, the turmoil and sadness, the jealousy and anger, melted away like a stick of sugar candy in hot tea.

She stared into his hazel eyes. The edge was gone from them now, leaving pools of molten brown, luminous and deep. Excitement, fear, joy, and every other emotion pooled out and filled her own heart.

"How can I return home without knowing you care?" he said at last.

"You don't have to."

The words tumbled out before she could stop them, but as she spoke, she realized she meant them with every part of her soul.

"How do you think Law and Fern would feel about a double wedding?" he asked softly.

Instead of answering, she tipped back her head. He took the invitation, and gave her a long, lingering kiss.

EPILOGUE

Dusk fell over the forest, and a loon called out from the pond, rising among the song of the spring peepers.

"Gale, come down!" A little girl in a frilly, lacy dress, with golden pigtails crossed over her back, called at the foot of the giant oak tree. "Your mother said it's too dark and you might miss a step!"

A lithe child with hair that billowed like a smoky cloud around her shoulders slid down the trunk and landed gracefully on the forest floor.

"Look at you," the golden-haired girl scolded. "Isn't that the third pinafore you've torn this week?"

Gale crossed her arms. "Zephyr don't scold. Mama doesn't mind mending them. You should have come up with me. The dove's eggs are going to hatch any day."

"I'll come tomorrow," Zephyr promised. "But I'll wait until

I'm wearing my play clothes. Mrs. Crenshaw said her fingers are worn to the bone from mending and I'll have to do it myself from now on."

Gail snorted. "I'd like to see that."

"I can mend just fine," Zephyr said primly. "But I'd much rather be out playing with you."

The two girls linked arms and moved down the well-worn path.

"What's dinner going to be at your house?" Gale asked.

"We've been invited to the ranch to eat with Grandpa," said Zephyr. "Suits me. Mrs. Crenshaw's a better cook than mama any day."

"She sure is." Gale stopped to pull up a droopy stocking. "I'll pop over the fence and ask mama if I can come to your house for supper."

"I'm sure Aunt Iris will let you come," Zephyr clasped her hands. "Ask if you can stay the night!" she called, as the dark head bobbed over the fence. "And mind your dress!" she cried.

"I will!" Gale called back.

SEASON OF FLIGHT

About the Author

Angela has been writing stories since she created her first book with a green crayon at the age of eight. She's lived all over Central Texas, mostly hovering in and around the small town of Bastrop Texas, which she loves with unnatural fierceness and features in many of her books. Angela has four wild children, a husband who studies astrophysics for fun, and a cat.

To find out more about her writing and learn how to receive a FREE short story, go to http://angelacastillowrites.weebly.com

Excerpt From

Where He Leads

Westward Wanderers
Book 1, Available on Amazon in
paperback, Kindle and Audible.
https://www.amazon.com/Westward-Wanderers-Book-
One-Christian-Historical-ebook/dp/B0813NV1KP

I
Unexpected Meetings

Ami hurried down the street, weaving through people lost in their own Tuesday errands. A peddler held out a silver hand-mirror for her inspection, and a little girl reached out a chubby hand to stroke the shimmering fabric of her dress.

"Don't touch, Abigail!" A woman jerked the child's hand away. "The fine lady doesn't want her gown soiled."

"She's not a bother." Ami touched the little girl's crimson cheek. "I might have done the same thing at her age."

A carriage flew past, much faster than prudent in the crowded square. Ami jumped to the side to miss a spray of sand and pebbles. "Oaf driver," she murmured.

She made her way to the butcher's shop and hesitated in front of the battered door. The building was always stuffy, smelly, and buzzing with flies. "Oh, why did I promise Nancy I'd check for lamb chops?" But the dish was her own favorite, so she held her breath and cracked the door open.

Before Ami could step inside, she noticed a woman rushing down the street. The woman's dress, filled with countless petticoats and a hoopskirt, billowed around her, dragging through the mud with no heed.

Ami paused as she recognized Martha Davis. The woman wasn't one for fancy clothes, since her family was considerably poorer than the Kents and a mother with seven children rarely had the time or need for such deportment. Ami's curiosity was piqued even further when Martha pushed the cumbersome skirts to one side and plopped down on a hitching block a few yards away, narrowly preventing her crinoline from being exposed to the street. The middle-aged woman fanned her red face with the sheaf of papers in her hand.

Ami ran to her, curiosity burning in her soul almost as fiercely as concern. "Dear Mrs. Davis, whatever has brought you to this state?"

Martha sucked in a breath and smiled. "Oh, hello, Ami. I hope you are well. This corset is quite constricting. Gave up wearing them three children ago. I don't know how I managed to put it on, and I'm certainly unsure I'll ever get out of the garment."

"Oh dear," was all Ami could think to say.

"I'll be fine," Mrs. Davis waved her papers. "However, I've returned from a meeting. Tom felt it prudent to look as respectable as could be managed. I've been to the bank, you see."

"I see," said Ami, though she didn't. Martha Davis had been her mother's closest friend and confidant, but Ami mostly only nodded to them at church since her mother's passing two years ago. The Davis family had lived a quiet life with few scandals in their history, so they remained out of town gossip for the most part. That is, until Mr. Davis had up and left town the year before.

"It's Tom," Mrs. Davis continued, swinging her feet, like a little girl would do, so her thick leather shoes thudded against the wooden surface. "As you probably know, he took my two oldest boys to Oregon last May, they're twelve and fourteen. They've been building our home on our land. Forty acres we have and every inch of it free. I was meant to bring the rest of the children out next year."

Ami gasped. "How courageous of you."

"Courageous or addled," Martha rolled her eyes. "Tom's

had to take on other work, trapping for pelts and the like, to pay for supplies and keep the boys' bellies full. Everything's more costly than we considered." She wiped a line of sweat from her forehead. "He's had to leave my boys alone for days at a time, and I don't like it. I've decided to go this spring instead of next year." She held out the top paper from her sheaf, and it shook in her fingers. "And here's the note from the bank."

Ami examined the bill of sale. "They bought your house?"

Mrs. Davis nodded. "The home belonged to my grandfather, so it's in my name. Wasn't a male heir." She sighed. "I wish I could have gone to Oregon when Tom went. But he left so soon after the war. Random Johnny Rebs still roaming. And me with a newborn babe in my arms." She tapped her chin. "Part of me hoped he'd change his mind and come trundling home. But he didn't. And if I ever want to see my boys again, I'll be braving the trail with my other children."

"Oh, Mrs. Davis." Ami struggled to find a comforting word, but imagination failed her.

"It's all right, dear." Mrs. Davis jumped down from the hitching block and gave her a bright smile. "Providence will see us through, sure as sure. I'm glad to have my Ellie.

Seventeen and sharp as a tack, but since her bout with scarlet fever last year, she's been waning. It'll be a struggle to keep four little un's bobbing along the trail in a straight line. I'd like to hire a girl to come along." She examined the papers in her hands. "But who'd gallivant away to Oregon, off the top?"

"I'm sure I don't know, Mrs. Davis." Ami suddenly remembered her errand. She took the woman's hand, damp with sweat. "I will remember you in my prayers. Every day, not only Sunday."

"Thank you, dearie." Mrs. Davis squeezed her fingers. "Call on me if you have a chance. I always love to see those kind brown eyes, so much like your mother's."

As Ami left the butcher's shop with her parcel, drops of rain, round and ripe, hit her with such force that she wondered if Mr. Gootleg's twin boys were throwing rotten tomatoes again. But after the first few spotted her dress and bonnet brim, the droplets turned into a torrential downpour.

She darted under a nearby saloon's awning and clutched her reticule tighter. Tucked inside was a sample of the glorious magenta silk she'd commissioned for her ball gown. Silk was worth a fortune, and most of the women in town would give their eye-teeth for such a scrap. Ami was well aware of this, but these thoughts always brought a mixture of emotions. A swell of pride for her father, who worked his way up from a child of Dutch immigrants to one of Missouri's finest builders. And an imagined scolding from her mother, who had been raised in an impoverished pastor's family and taught her not to put on airs.

She brushed a tear from her cheek that had mixed with the rain. Though Mama had been buried and gone for two years now, certain memories still sent tiny pinpricks to her soul. During the funeral, the pastor had said Mama was looking down from a cloud with the angels, but Ami hated the thought of her being so far away. Too distant to see what went on in Ami's life, and too far to hear when she said a quick hello. Which might be scandalous. *Is speaking to a dead loved one blasphemous?* She'd long since stopped trying to ask Reverend Balder these questions. He was mortified by her forwardness and instead of answering, always assigned her memory verses that had nothing to do with the original inquiry.

Rain fell in sheets now, and she couldn't stay in front of the saloon. Anyone who saw her there would surely traipse off to Millany to report. Her stepmother had eyes and ears all over town.

My second-best bonnet shall be ruined. A dandy one, with bits of ostrich plume imported from Darkest Africa and snippets of ribbon from the upcoming ball gown. Dorothy Anne, her dressmaker and dearest friend, would be so upset.

As the rain relented for a moment, a yawning entryway across from the saloon beckoned to her. She hurried through the now ankle-deep rivulets of water that rushed down the street in miniature torrents.

At least she'd had the presence of mind to wear riding boots instead of her calling slippers. The more sensible footwear ushered her to safety, and she ducked into the cavernous building, unsure of her fortuitous sanctuary.

The rich scent of soaped leather and hay greeted her nose. Horses snorted greetings from a row of stalls.

The livery stable. Of course. Ami hiked up her bedraggled skirts and went to the closest steed.

"Hello there. Aren't you a beauty?" she crooned to a massive black stallion with a bright blaze across his muzzle. She scooped a handful of oats and lifted them up. The stallion picked each oat from her outstretched palm with velvety lips.

"Looks like General fancies you." A tall, slender man with a thick black mustache strode through the door. He tipped the edge of his bowler hat. "Good afternoon, ma'am."

Ami pressed her fingers against her shirt front. "Goodness, you gave me a start." Her hands flew to her bedraggled hat. "Pardon me. I slipped in to escape the deluge."

The man held out a gloved hand. "General and I are glad you did. Name's Paul Amos."

"Amethyst Kent. But everyone calls me Ami." Ami placed her hand in his, and Paul brushed it with a kiss.

A tingle ran down Ami's arm.

Paul let go of her hand and strode over to General. "Rain appears to be letting up. I'm planning to hitch General to my carriage," he gestured to a small buggy nearby. "I'm on my way out of town, but if you like, I could give you a ride home."

"That would be lovely." Ami's heart flip-flopped in her chest. *Would it be prudent to take a ride home from a stranger? He's obviously a gentleman.* She raised her chin. *I am nineteen, after all. I'm old enough to make up my own mind. And home's fifteen minutes away. Barely a wink and a nod until we get there.*

Paul smiled. "Bear with me, it takes a while to get him settled. There's a crate right there if you'd care to sit a spell." He waved a gloved hand at the mentioned item.

"Goodness no, I'll help you with the tack." Ami waltzed over to the buggy to check the shafts. "I spend a lot of time in my father's stables. Our groom, Ol' Pat, has taught me everything there is to know about horses. He says I could ride before I took my first step."

"Ah." Paul turned from the stall. "How does your husband feel about you spending your days riding?"

Ami let out a short laugh. "He'd be hard pressed to have a say in the matter, since he doesn't exist."

Paul arched one aristocratic eyebrow. "Yes, that would make it a bit difficult."

Ami leaned on a stand before her, resting her chin in her hands. "Mister's my best friend. He'd be lonely if I didn't spend time with him."

"Mister?" Paul darted her a slanted glance.

"My bay thoroughbred. Couple of hands smaller than General, but he's a beauty."

"I'm sure he is." Paul led General out of the stall and began running his palms down the massive, gleaming legs. "As you can see, I fixed the harness before finding my breakfast at the inn. I need to check him for swelling, we travelled a long way yesterday."

"Oh?" Ami felt it rude to ask for more information, though questions swam through her mind. Surely she'd have heard if someone from town was expecting a handsome gentleman visitor.

"Yes." Paul finished with the last leg and led the horse to the buggy's shafts. "Back up, boy. There's a good one."

The horse did as he was told as meekly as a Sunday school teacher. Ami smiled. *A pleasure to see a man who knows how to work with horses.*

She fastened the shaft on one side while Paul worked on the other. Captain tossed his mane and gave tiny whickers.

"That's it then." Paul came over to her side and gave a few tugs on the traces. "Snug as a bug. Let's get you home, Miss Kent."

She took his offered hand and sprang into the gleaming leather seat. That same tremor ran through her at his touch, even through their gloves.

"The trip home isn't long," she said, trying to keep the regret from her voice.

"At least the ride will save your skirts from further ruin." He gestured to her dress, where the mud and damp had already crept up the hem by several inches.

"Oh, yes. Thank you." Brenda, her personal maid, would be horrified as it was. But the shower truly had come out of a perfectly clear sky. It wasn't as though she'd meant to get soaked. Besides, these things always seemed to happen to her and Brenda was a dear soul who loved her no matter what.

As the buggy trundled into the street, a bit of chill air hit the wet spots on Ami's dress and she was tempted to scoot just a few inches closer to the handsome Paul Amos. But she shook her head. *You scandalous thing, you! Millany would be appalled.*

Not that it wouldn't be fun to see her father's second wife's shocked expression. *She'll already be mad about me ruining my clothes. Better not throw fuel into the fire.* Most of her encounters with Millany in the last few weeks had been fraught with tight-lipped tension on both sides. It was a good thing Amy would be going to Sasha Regent's coming out ball in a month. *We need a rest from each other.*

Paul rubbed the back of his neck. "I just realized you haven't told me where you live,"

"Oh, goodness, how silly of me! You're headed in the right direction. I live south of town, on Granbury Street."

"You'll have to direct me." Paul settled back in his seat. "I'm new to these parts. Passing through, really."

"Oh?" Ami tried to emphasize the question a bit, hoping he would take the hint.

"Yes." He rested his elbow lazily on the back of the buggy seat.

She held her breath, wondering if he'd be so forward as to put his arm around her, but he didn't.

"I'm heading to Independence. I intend to sell my buggy and join an outfit for Oregon."

"Oh." The little castles in the air Ami had begun to build

came crashing down in heaps of rubble. Oregon was a lifetime away. And unless you counted teamsters and scouts, the folks who went down that trail never came back. "You're the second person today to tell me they've decided on that particular venture."

"There's fortunes to be had and land to be settled," Paul said. He adjusted the reins that he'd wrapped around his whip. "And it's our God-given duty to claim the land with civilized boots, wouldn't you say?"

Ami stared down at Paul's meticulously polished boots and tried to imagine him as a settler of new lands, but the idea didn't quite measure up. She murmured something in assent and then became quiet for the rest of the trip, only answering yes or no to Paul's cheerful babble or pointing out the correct direction when they reached a fork in the road. By the time her father's stately home and grounds appeared over the horizon, the sun streamed over the front lawn, and raindrops sparkled on bright April grass.

"This is my home." She waved her hand towards the gate.

He stopped the buggy on the drive, came around and helped her step down. "Mind the mud, it's still thick here," he said.

"Thank you for the ride, Mr. Amos." Ami shook his hand. "Be careful on your trip."

"Course I will," said Paul. "If you're ever in Oregon, you could come and ride with me again."

Ami couldn't help but chuckle at the absurdity of his statement. "I'll do that," she replied. An invitation to luncheon rested on her lips, but she'd already been too forward, too brazen, by accepting a ride in the first place.

With nothing more to say but "Goodbye and thank you," Ami uttered both phrases in haste and trudged down the sodden drive to the courtyard, her voluminous skirts growing heavier by the step.

As Ami rushed in, she passed Millany.

The tall, stately woman pressed her hand on a pane of glass in the drawing room window that ran from floor to ceiling. No other home in Memphis had a window so large, with four-and-twenty sections and the top four made of red colored glass. Mama had loved the window, but Ami had always felt a bit afraid of the room because in the morning sun, the light shining through the top panes seemed to her like blood streaming over the white pine floor.

Millany wore her house dress, a green taffeta, which was only slightly less grand than the dresses she chose for calling.

It rustled like leaves in the fall as she turned to face Ami, looking for all the world like an exotic plant, her titian hair dressed in a flaming pompadour at the top.

Her pale cheeks reddened. "Amethyst Kent! Where have you been? And what happened to your dress?"

Ami bit her lip, ruing her decision to enter through the front and not the servant's door. She wasn't afraid of her stepmother. After all, Millany had been her school mate and only four forms ahead. At eight years of age Ami had whipped her in a fight when Millany had mocked her for spelling 'miscreant' incorrectly. Ever since then, the two had been at odds and Millany's introduction to the Kent household had only worsened the problem.

Millany did everything she could to make Ami's life miserable, but when Ami's father was home she played the victim, creating elaborate descriptions of the wrongs Ami had committed. Father often berated Ami, despite her protests, and then left the scene, commanding the 'women work out their differences."

This evening, Ami simply didn't wish to endure any sort of conflict after the heartsick disappointment she'd experienced mere moments before. *And I WILL be heartsick,* she answered her own admonishment. Paul Amos was as goodly as any eligible man she'd met in Memphis, and there were precious few of those in the first place. *Why didn't I invite him to lunch?*

"You look a fright." Millany's voice shook. "Your father's perfectly good money poured into a dress and you've ruined it. And furthermore," she turned, her hands clenched at her sides, "I can't believe you'd allow yourself to be seen in that state. What will my friends say?"

Ami rolled her eyes. Her stepmother's focus in life was looks, fashion, and what everyone else thought. She didn't care what had to be done or who must be hurt to get what she wanted, in any situation.

"I was caught in the sudden shower, Millany. I didn't intend to ruin my dress today, but you have nothing to fret over. I'm fairly sure your friends all stayed in their homes to prevent their sugar-spun souls from melting."

Millany turned back to her brooding stance at the window, her lips in a tight line.

Though she spoke not a word, Ami knew what she was thinking, for she'd overheard Millany say it to a friend. "The girl is common, as her mother was common, for all her father's wealth. Can't make a silk purse from a sow's ear."

Ami shook away the irritation she always felt when she remembered that conversation. No matter how hard she tried, she'd never be good enough for her stepmother. She was weary of the attempt.

Millany snapped her head back as quick as a rattlesnake. "I'm vexed with you. Leave my sight."

Biting back a flood of angry words, Ami rushed up the stairs as fast as she was able.

As Ami reached her room, she rang a little servant's bell. She'd barely had time to undress before Brenda's familiar plodding steps approached her door.

The maid popped her head in. "Will you be needing a bath drawn then, Miss Ami?"

"Yes, please, Brenda." Ami gestured to a pile of sodden clothing bundled on a chair. "And I'm afraid my clothes are a mess. I got caught in the sudden shower today."

"Your best dimity." Brenda shook her head until her lace cap rustled. "This is going to take a sight of washing, and I'm not sure I'll ever be able to get the train back to snowy again."

"I know, and I'm sorry." Ami perched on the low-lying window seat in her chemise and bloomers. "I don't know what possessed me to ask for a train in that color. Dorothy Anne raised an eyebrow, but she didn't say anything. I wish she'd warned me."

"Probably worried you'd throw one of those rich folks temper tantrums." Brenda chuckled.

Ami's mouth fell open. "Brenda, I would never."

Brenda picked up Ami's muddy boots and placed them outside her door. "No, your mother wouldn't have stood for it. She raised you right, your mother did. She wasn't nothing like Mrs. Fancy Missy out there."

Ami folded her arms tight over her chest. She and Brenda moaned about their common dislike for Millany often. The tension that arose between stepmother and stepdaughter was stifling, and Ami often placated Millany's ridiculous demands simply to keep the peace. *Mother wouldn't have wanted us to live in a house of strife.*

###

That night, Ami blew out her lamps and snuggled down under her feather coverlet. Thoughts of Paul rose over all others in her mind. His confident smile. His infectious laugh. He was the kind of man who'd have women hanging on to his every word at a dinner party.

He's going to Oregon, she kept telling herself. *He'll probably die of dysentery anyway, or get gut-shot by a raider.*

But she stayed awake far longer than she'd ever admit to a living soul, dreaming of a handsome man in a bowler hat.

ANGELA CASTILLO

Excerpt From

The River Girl's Song

Texas Women of Spirit
Book 1, Available on Amazon in
paperback, Kindle and audio.

http://www.amazon.com/The-River-Girls-Song-Spirit-ebook/dp/B00X32KBL0/ref=pd_rhf_gw_p_img_1?ie=UTF8&refRID=18DCQ0M4FSR2VYKTRJ15

1
Scarlet Sunset

"We need to sharpen these knives again." Zillia examined her potato in the light from the window. Peeling took so long with a dull blade, and Mama had been extra fond of mash this month.

Mama poured cream up to the churn's fill line and slid the top over the dasher. "Yes, so many things to do! And we'll be even busier in a few weeks." She began to churn the butter, her arms stretched out to avoid her swollen belly. "Don't fret. Everything will settle into place."

"Tell that to Jeb when he comes in, hollering for his dinner," muttered Zillia. The potato turned into tiny bits beneath her knife.

"Don't be disrespectful." Though Mama spoke sharply, her mouth quirked up into a smile. She leaned over to examine Zillia's work. "Watch your fingers."

"Sorry, I wasn't paying attention." Zillia scooped the potato bits into the kettle and pulled another one out of the bag. Her long, slender fingers already bore several scars reaped by impatience.

"Ooh, someone's kicking pretty hard today." Mama rubbed her stomach.

Zillia looked away. When Papa was alive, she would have given anything for a little brother or sister. In the good times, the farm had prospered, and she chose new shoes from a catalogue every year. Ice was delivered in the summer and firewood came in two loads at the beginning of winter. Back then, Mama could have hired a maid to help out when the little one came.

She and Mama spent most of their time working together, and they discussed everything. But she didn't dare talk about those days. Mama always cried.

"I might need you to finish this." Mama stopped for a moment and wiped her face with her muslin apron. "I'm feeling a little dizzy."

"Why don't you sit down, and I'll make you some tea?" Zillia put down her knife and went to wash her hands in the basin.

Water, streaked with red, gushed from beneath Mama's petticoats. She gasped, stepped back and stared at the growing puddle on the floor. "Oh dear. I'm guessing it's time."

"Are you sure? Dr. Madison said you had weeks to go." Zillia had helped with plenty of births on the farm, but only for animals. From what she'd gathered, human babies brought far more fuss and trouble. She shook the water off her hands and went to her mother's side.

Mama sagged against Zillia's shoulder, almost throwing her off balance. She moaned and trembled. The wide eyes staring into Zillia's did not seem like they could belong to the prim, calm woman who wore a lace collar at all times, even while milking the goats.

Zillia steadied herself with one hand on the kitchen table. "We need to get you to a comfortable place. Does it hurt terribly?"

Mama's face relaxed and she stood a little straighter. "Sixteen years have passed since I went through this with you, but I remember." She wiped her eyes. "We have a while to go, don't be frightened. Just go tell your stepfather to fetch the doctor."

Zillia frowned, the way she always did when anyone referred to the man her mother married as her stepfather. Jeb had not been her choice and was no kin to her. "Let me help you into bed first."

They moved in slow, shaky steps through the kitchen and into Mama's bedroom. Zillia hoped Mama couldn't feel her frenzied heartbeat. *I have no right to be afraid; it's not me who has to bring an entire baby into this world.*

Red stains crept up the calico hem of Mama's skirts as they dragged on the floor.

A sourness rose in the back of Zillia's throat. *This can't be right.* "Is it supposed to be such a mess?"

"Oh yes." Mama gave a weak chuckle. "And much more to come. Wait until you meet the new little one. It's always worth the trouble."

Mama grasped her arm when they reached the large bed, covered in a cheery blue and white quilt. "Before you go, help me get this dress off. Please?"

Zillia's hands shook so much she could hardly unfasten the buttons. It seemed like hours before she was able to get all forty undone, from Mama's lower back to the nape of her neck. She peeled the dress off the quivering shoulders, undoing the stays and laces until only the thin lace slip was left.

Another spasm ran through Mama's body. She hunched over and took several deep breaths. After a moment, she collected herself and stumbled out of the pile of clothing.

When Zillia gathered the dress to the side, she found a larger pool of blood under the cloth. Thin streams ran across the wood to meet the sunlight waning through the windowpanes. "There's so much blood, Mama, how can we make it stop?"

"Nothing can stop a baby coming. We just have to do the best we can and pray God will see us through." "I know, Mama, but can't you see... I don't know what to do." Zillia rubbed her temples and stepped back.

Mama's mouth was drawn, and she stared past Zillia, like she wasn't there.

Mama won't want the bed ruined. Zillia pulled the quilt off the feather tick and set it aside. A stack of cloths had been stored beneath the wash basin in preparation for this day. She spread them out over the mattress and helped her mother roll onto the bed.

Thin blue veins stood out on Mama's forehead. She squeezed her eyes shut. "Go out and find Jeb, like I told you. Then get some water boiling and come back in here as fast as you can."

Zillia grabbed her sunbonnet and headed out the door. "God, please, please let him be close. And please make him listen to me," she said aloud, like she usually prayed.

Parts of her doubted the Almighty God cared to read her thoughts, so she'd speak prayers when no one else could hear. At times she worried some busybody would find out and be scandalized by her lack of faith, but unless they could read thoughts, how would they know?

None of the urgency and fear enclosed in the house had seeped into the outside world. Serene pine trees, like teeth on a broken comb, lined the bluff leading to the Colorado River. Before her, stalks littered the freshly harvested cornfield, stretching into the distance. Chickens scattered as she rushed across the sunbaked earth, and goats bounded to the fence, sharp eyes watching for treats.

"Let Jeb be close!" she prayed again, clutching her sunbonnet strings in both fists. She hurried to the barn. Her mother's husband had spent the last few days repairing the goat fence, since the little rascals always found ways to escape. But he'd wanted to check over the back field today.

Sounds of iron striking wood came from inside. She released the breath she'd been holding and stepped into the gloomy barn.

Jeb's back was towards her, his shirt soaked through. Late summer afternoon. A terrible time for chores in Texas, and the worst time to be swollen with child, Mama said.

"Jeb, Mama says it's time. Please go get the doctor."

"Wha-at?" Jeb snarled. He always snarled when her mother wasn't around. He swung the axe hard into a log so it bit deep and stuck. The man turned and wiped the sweat from his thin, red face. Brown snakes of hair hung down to his shoulders in unkempt strands. "I got a whole day of work left and here it is, almost sunset. I don't have time to ride into town for that woman's fits and vapors. She ain't due yet."

Zillia fought for a reply. She couldn't go for the doctor herself; she'd never leave Mama alone.

Jeb reached for the axe.

"There's blood all over the floor. She says it's time, so it's time." Zillia tried to speak with authority, like Mama when she wanted to get a point across. "You need to go Jeb. Get going now."

When it came to farm work, Jeb moved like molasses. But the slap came so fast Zillia had no time to duck or defend herself. She fell to the ground and held her face. Skin burned under her fingers. "Please, Jeb, please go for help!" she pleaded. Though he'd threatened her before, he'd never struck her.

"Shut up!" Jeb growled. "I'll go where and when I wish. No girl's gonna tell me what to do." He moved away, and she heard the horse nicker as he entered the stable.

Wooden walls swirled around Zillia's head. The anger and fear that coursed through her system overcame the pain and she pushed herself up and stood just in time to see Jeb riding down the road in the direction of the farm belonging to their closest neighbors, the Eckhart family.

They can get here faster than the doctor. First common sense thing the man's done all day. "Please God," she prayed again. "Please let Grandma Louise and Soonie be home."

Blood, scarlet like the garnets on Mama's first wedding ring, seemed to cover everything. The wooden floor slats. Linen sheets, brought in a trunk when their family came from Virginia. Zillia's fingers, all white and stained with the same sticky blood, holding Mama's as though they belonged to one hand.

The stench filled the room, sending invisible alarms to her brain. Throughout the birth, they had played in her head. *This can't be right. This can't be right.*\

The little mite had given them quite a tug of war, every bit as difficult as the goats when they twinned. Finally he'd come, covered in slippery blood that also gushed around him.

Over in a cradle given to them by a woman from church, the baby waved tiny fists in the air. His lips opened and his entire face became his mouth, in a mighty scream for one so small. Zillia had cleared his mouth and nose to make sure he could breathe, wrapped him in a blanket, and gone back to her mother's side.

Mama's breaths came in ragged gasps. Her eyelids where closed but her eyes moved under the lids, as though she had the fever. Zillia pressed her mother's hand up to her own forehead, mindless of the smear of red it would leave behind.

The burned sun shrank behind the line of trees. No fire or lantern had been lit to stave off the darkness, but Zillia was too weary to care. Her spirits sank as her grasp on Mama's hand tightened.

At some point Mama's screams had turned into little moans and sobs, and mutterings Zillia couldn't understand. How long had it been since they'd spoken? The only clock in the house was on the kitchen mantle, but by the light Zillia figured an hour or more had passed since Jeb left. When the bloody tide had ebbed at last, Zillia wasn't sure if the danger was over, or if her mother simply didn't have more to bleed.

A knock came at the door. The sound she had waited and prayed for, what seemed like all her life. "Please come in." The words came in hoarse sections, as though she had to remind herself how to speak.

The door squeaked open and cool evening air blew through the room, a blessed tinge of relief from the stifling heat.

"Zillia, are you in here?" A tall, tan girl stepped into the room, carrying a lantern. Her golden-brown eyes darted from the mess, to the bed, to the baby in the cradle. "Oh, Zillia, Jeb met Grandma and me in town and told us to come. I thought Mrs. Bowen had weeks to go, yet." She set the light on the bedside table and rushed over to check the baby, her moccasins padding on the wooden floor.

"No doctor, Soonie?" Zillia croaked.

"Doctor Madison was delivering a baby across the river, and something's holding up the ferry. We passed Jeb at the dock, that's when he told us what was going on. The horses couldn't move any faster. I thought Grandma was going to unhitch the mare and ride bareback to get here."

In spite of the situation, Zillia's face cracked into a smile at the thought of tiny, stout Grandma Louise galloping in from town.

An old woman stepped in behind Soonie. Though Grandma Louise wasn't related to Zillia by blood, close friends called her 'grandma' anyway. She set down a bundle of blankets. A wrinkled hand went to her mouth while she surveyed the room, but when she caught Zillia's eye she gave a capable smile. "I gathered everything I could find from around the house and pulled the pot from the fire so we could get this little one cleaned up." She bustled over to the bedside. "Zillia, why don't you go in the kitchen and fill a washtub with warm water?"

Though Zillia heard the words, she didn't move. She might never stir again. For eternity she would stay in this place, willing her mother to keep breathing.

"Come on, girl." Grandma Louise tugged her arm, then stopped when she saw the pile of stained sheets. Her faded blue eyes watered.

Zillia blinked. "Mama, we have help." *Maybe everything will be all right.*

Grandma Louise had attended births for years before a doctor had come to Bastrop. She tried to pull Zillia's hand away from her mother's, but her fingers stuck.

Mama's eyes fluttered. "Zillia, my sweet girl. Where is my baby? Is he all right?"

Soonie gathered the tiny bundle in her arms and brought him over. "He's a pretty one, Mrs. Bowen. Ten fingers and toes, and looks healthy."

A smile tugged at one corner of Mama's pale lips. "He is pink and plump. Couldn't wish for more."

Grandma Louise came and touched Mama's forehead. "We're here now, Marjorie."

Mama's chest rose, and her exhaled breath rattled in her throat. Her eyes never left Zillia's face. "You'll do fine. Just fine. Don't—" She gasped once more, and her eyes closed.

Zillia had to lean forward to catch the words.

"Don't tell Jeb about the trunk."

"Mama?" Zillia grabbed the hand once more, but the strength had already left her mother's fingers. She tugged at her mother's arm, but it dropped back, limp on the quilt.

A tear trickled down Grandma Louise's wrinkled cheek. "Go on to the kitchen, Zillia. The baby should be nearer to the fire with this night air comin' on. Soonie and I will clean up in here."

"I don't want to leave her," Zillia protested. But one glance at her mother's face and the world seemed to collapse around her, like the woodpile when she didn't stack it right.

How could Mama slip away? A few hours ago they'd been laughing while the hens chased a grasshopper through the yard. They'd never spent a night apart and now Mama had left for another world all together. She pulled her hand back and stood to her feet. She blinked, wondering what had caused her to make such a motion.

Soonie held the baby out. His eyes, squinted shut from crying, opened for a moment and she caught a hint of blue. Blue like Mama's.

Zillia took him in her arms. Her half-brother was heavier then he looked, and so warm. She tucked the cloth more tightly around him while he squirmed to get free. "I have to give him a bath." Red fingerprints dotted the blanket. "I need to wash my hands."

"Of course you do. Let's go see if the water is heated and we'll get you both cleaned up." Tears brimmed in Soonie's eyes and her lip trembled, but she picked the bundle of cloths that Grandma Louise had gathered and led the way into the kitchen, her smooth, black braid swinging to her waist as she walked.

Zillia cradled the baby in one arm, and her other hand strayed to her tangled mess of hair that had started the day as a tidy bun with ringlets in the front. What would Mama say? She stopped short while Soonie checked the water and searched for a washtub. *Mama will never say anything. Ever again.*

The baby began to wail again, louder this time, and her gulping sobs fell down to meet his.

Zillia sank to the floor, where she and the baby cried together until the bath had been prepared.

As Soonie wrapped the clean baby in a fresh blanket, Jeb burst into the house. He leaned against the door. "The doctor's on his way." His eyes widened when he saw the baby. "That's it, then? Boy or girl?"

"Boy." Soonie rose to her feet. "Jeb, where have you been? I saw you send someone else across on the ferry."

Jeb licked his lips and stared down at the floor. "Well, ah, I got word to the doctor. I felt a little thirsty, thought I'd celebrate. I mean, birthing is women's work, right?"

The bedroom door creaked open, and Grandma Louise stepped into the kitchen. Strands of gray hair had escaped her simple arrangement. Her eyes sparked in a way Zillia had only witnessed a few times, and knew shouldn't be taken lightly.

"Your thirst has cost you dearly, Jeb Bowen." Grandma Louise's Swedish accent grew heavier, as it always did with strong emotion. "While you drank the Devil's brew, your wife bled out her last hours. You could have spared a moment to bid her farewell. After all, she died to bring your child into the world."

Jeb stepped closer to Grandma Louise, and his lips twitched. Zillia knew he fought to hold back the spew of foul words she and her mother had been subjected to many times. Whether from shock or some distant respect for the elderly woman, he managed to keep silent while he pushed past Grandma Louise and into the bedroom.

Zillia stepped in behind him. Somehow, in the last quarter of an hour, Grandma Louise had managed to scrub away the worst of the blood and dispose of the stained sheets and petticoats. The blue quilt was smoothed over her mother's body, almost to her chin. Her hands where folded over her chest, like she always held them in church during prayer.

Tears threatened to spill out, but Zillia held them back. She wouldn't cry in front of Jeb.

The man reached over and touched Mama's cheek, smoothing a golden curl back into place above her forehead. "You was a good woman, Marjorie," he muttered.

"Jeb." Zillia stretched out her hand, but she didn't dare to touch him.

When he turned, his jaws were slack, and his eyes had lost their normal fire. "You stupid girl. Couldn't even save her."

Zillia flinched. A blow would have been better. *Surely the man isn't completely addled? Not even the doctor could have helped Mama.* She shrank back against the wall, and swallowed words dangerous to her own self.

Jeb stared at her for another moment, then bowed his head. "I guess that's that." He turned on his boot and walked out of the room.

Find out more about this book, and Angela Castillo's other writings, at http://angelacastillowrites.weebly.com

Made in the USA
Middletown, DE
05 February 2022